James M. Cain

The Postman
Always Rings Twice

ORION

To Vincent Lawrence

This edition produced for The Book People Ltd,
Hall Wood Avenue, Haydock, St Helens, WA11 9UL

An Orion paperback

First published in the United States of America in 1934
by Alfred A. Knopf, Inc.
This paperback edition published in 2005
by Orion Books Ltd,
Orion House, 5 Upper St Martin's Lane,
London WC2H 9EA

A CIP catalogue record for this book is available
from the British Library.

ISBN 9781407213316

Typeset at SetSystems
Printed and bound in Great Britain by
Clays Ltd, St Ives plc

www.orionbooks.co.uk

A word on James M. Cain by James Lee Burke

I discovered the novels of James M. Cain late in my writing career. As a boy during the 1940s, I had seen two or three of the motion pictures based on his work, but I had never read the books themselves nor had I associated Cain's name with any notable contribution to American writing. Finally, on a whim, I read *The Postman Always Rings Twice*. I was stunned. I went to a major chain store and tried to buy his other novels. None was in the store's inventory and I had to order them.

By the time I had finished *Mildred Pierce* and *Double Indemnity*, I could not believe I had gone so long in my own career without discovering the work of this fine writer. But looking back upon my years of undergraduate and graduate work, and the twenty-six years I spent teaching in various American colleges, I do not remember one reference on the part of anyone, teacher or student or colleague, to the name of James M. Cain. This may be due to the fact that it has been the long-ingrained view of academics that the unpardonable sin for an artist is to achieve monetary success in his own lifetime, particularly through the influence of Hollywood. Or perhaps literary success and recognition have been always fickle in nature, and the career of James M. Cain was no different from that of his contemporaries F. Scott Fitzgerald and A. B. Guthrie.

Ultimately the failure of discovery was mine. Cain was a master craftsman. The very fact that three of his novels could be adapted so easily to the screen should have indicated to me the strength of his storyline and the originality and crispness of his dialogue. Rarely do books become fine films by accident. But perhaps an even more important element in Cain's work and its successful film adaptation is the complexity of his characters. They're the denizens of what we today call a 'crime novel', but by and large they are ordinary people, much like ourselves. Their tragedy, according to Cain's own statement, is that they get what they want, which he considered the worst fate that could befall human beings.

During the height of his career, critics talked about the influence of Ernest Hemingway and Dashiell Hammett upon Cain's prose. Cain was not complimented. He pointed out that he had written and published for years without reading either Hammett or Hemingway and that the origins of his stories and the formation of his prose style lay in his own experience as a journalist, a coal miner, and a soldier in the Great War. When asked if he was a member of the hardboiled school of detective writing, he replied he was not a member of a hardboiled school or, for that matter, a school of any kind.

His writing was not political, nor was it marked by the didacticism and proletarian themes of Depression literature. But like John Steinbeck and James T. Farrell, his thumb was on the pulse of people who worked in the fields, hitched the highways, waited tables in greasy spoons, and labored deep inside Appalachia coal mines. His characters believed with the fervor of religious converts that failure to achieve the American Dream, in matters of both money and the heart, was a form of secular sin. So, in a perverse way, unbeknown to themselves, his characters commit crimes to satisfy a value system that was invented for them by others.

But much of Cain's artistic gift, I think, lay in his ability to see and render everyday experience in a dramatic and interesting way. William Dean Howells once described a strange epiphany he experienced while riding a street car in late nineteenth-century Boston. It was dusk, the end of a hard day for the working people jammed on the car, and as Howells looked at the fatigue in their seamed faces, he wondered how the suffering and struggle of their lives did not burn through their skin like a flame burning through tallow.

Cain's aesthetic is almost like an emanation of Howells's

account. Cain saw meaning and dimension in the commonplace. The image seemed to travel from his eye through his arm and hand onto the paper as cleanly as light travels from the camera lens onto film. I think he heard Shakespeare's sound and fury in situations where others might only hear silence. I wish I had discovered him sooner. I don't think anyone could find a better writer to learn from.

They threw me off the hay truck about noon. I had swung on the night before, down at the border, and as soon as I got up there under the canvas, I went to sleep. I needed plenty of that, after three weeks in Tia Juana, and I was still getting it when they pulled off to one side to let the engine cool. Then they saw a foot sticking out and threw me off. I tried some comical stuff, but all I got was a dead pan, so that gag was out. They gave me a cigarette, though, and I hiked down the road to find something to eat.

That was when I hit this Twin Oaks Tavern. It was nothing but a roadside sandwich joint, like a million others in California. There was a lunchroom part, and over that a house part, where they lived, and off to one side a filling station, and out back a half dozen shacks that they called an auto court. I blew in there in a hurry and began looking down the road. When the Greek showed, I asked if a guy had been by in a Cadillac. He was to pick me up here, I said, and we were to have lunch. Not today, said the Greek. He laid a place at one of the tables and asked me what I was going to have. I said orange juice, corn flakes, fried eggs and bacon, enchilada, flapjacks, and coffee. Pretty soon he came out with the orange juice and the corn flakes.

'Hold on, now. One thing I got to tell you. If this guy

don't show up, you'll have to trust me for it. This was to be on him, and I'm kind of short, myself.'

'Hokay, fill'm up.'

I saw he was on, and quit talking about the guy in the Cadillac. Pretty soon I saw he wanted something.

'What you do, what kind of work, hey?'

'Oh, one thing and another, one thing and another. Why?'

'How old you?'

'Twenty-four.'

'Young fellow, hey? I could use young fellow right now. In my business.'

'Nice place you got here.'

'Air. Is a nice. No fog, like in a Los Angeles. No fog at all. Nice, a clear, all a time nice a clear.'

'Must be swell at night. I can smell it now.'

'Sleep fine. You understand automobile? Fix'm up?'

'Sure. I'm a born mechanic.'

He gave me some more about the air, and how healthy he's been since he bought this place, and how he can't figure it out, why his help won't stay with him. I can figure it out, but I stay with the grub.

'Hey? You think you like it here?'

By that time I had put down the rest of the coffee, and lit the cigar he gave me. 'I tell you how it is. I got a couple of other propositions, that's my trouble. But I'll think about it. I sure will do that all right.'

Then I saw her. She had been out back, in the kitchen, but she came in to gather up my dishes. Except for the shape, she really wasn't any raving beauty, but she had a sulky look to her, and her lips stuck out in a way that made me want to mash them in for her.

'Meet my wife.'

She didn't look at me. I nodded at the Greek, gave my cigar a kind of wave, and that was all. She went out with the dishes, and so far as he and I were concerned, she hadn't even been there. I left, then, but in five minutes I was back, to leave a message for the guy in the Cadillac. It took me a half hour to get sold on the job, but at the end of it I was in the filling station, fixing flats.

'What's your name, hey?'

'Frank Chambers.'

'Nick Papadakis, mine.'

We shook hands, and he went. In a minute I heard him singing. He had a swell voice. From the filling station I could just get a good view of the kitchen.

2

About three o'clock a guy came along that was all burned up because somebody had pasted a sticker on his wind wing. I had to go in the kitchen to steam it off for him.

'Enchiladas? Well, you people sure know how to make them.'

'What do you mean, you people?'

'Why, you and Mr Papadakis. You and Nick. That one I had for lunch, it was a peach.'

'Oh.'

'You got a cloth? That I can hold on to this thing with?'

'That's not what you meant.'

'Sure it is.'

'You think I'm Mex.'

'Nothing like it.'

'Yes, you do. You're not the first one. Well, get this. I'm just as white as you are, see? I may have dark hair and look a little that way, but I'm just as white as you are. You want to get along good around here, you won't forget that.'

'Why, you don't look Mex.'

'I'm telling you. I'm just as white as you are.'

'No, you don't look even a little bit Mex. Those Mexican women, they all got big hips and bum legs and breasts up under their chin and yellow skin and hair that looks like it had bacon fat on it. You don't look like that. You're small, and got nice white skin, and your hair is soft and curly, even if it is black. Only thing you've got that's Mex is your teeth. They all got white teeth, you've got to hand that to them.'

'My name was Smith before I was married. That don't sound much like a Mex, does it?'

'Not much.'

'What's more, I don't even come from around here. I come from Iowa.'

'Smith, hey. What's your first name?'

'Cora. You can call me that, if you want to.'

I knew for certain, then, what I had just taken a chance on when I went in there. It wasn't those enchiladas that she had to cook, and it wasn't having black hair. It was being married to that Greek that made her feel she wasn't white, and she was even afraid I would begin calling her Mrs Papadakis.

'Cora. Sure. And how about calling me Frank?'

She came over and began helping me with the wind wing. She was so close I could smell her. I shot it right close to her ear, almost in a whisper. 'How come you married this Greek, anyway?'

She jumped like I had cut her with a whip. 'Is that any of your business?'

'Yeah. Plenty.'

'Here's your wind wing.'

'Thanks.'

I went out. I had what I wanted. I had socked one in under her guard, and socked it in deep, so it hurt. From now on, it would be business between her and me. She might not say yes, but she wouldn't stall me. She knew what I meant, and she knew I had her number.

That night at supper, the Greek got sore at her for not giving me more fried potatoes. He wanted me to like it there, and not walk out on him like the others had.

'Give a man something to eat.'

'They're right on the stove. Can't he help himself?'

'It's all right. I'm not ready yet.'

He kept at it. If he had had any brains, he would have known there was something back of it, because she wasn't one to let a guy help himself, I'll say that for her. But he was dumb, and kept crabbing. It was just the kitchen table, he at one end, she at the other, and me in the middle. I didn't look at her. But I could see her dress. It was one of these white nurse uniforms, like they all wear, whether they work in a dentist's office or a bakeshop. It had been clean in the morning, but it was a little bit rumpled now, and mussy. I could smell her.

'Well for heaven's sake.'

She got up to get the potatoes. Her dress fell open for a second, so I could see her leg. When she gave me the potatoes, I couldn't eat. 'Well there now. After all that. and now he doesn't want them.'

'Hokay. But he have'm, *if* he want'm.'

'I'm not hungry. I ate a big lunch.'

He acted like he had won a great victory, and now he would forgive her, like the big guy he was. 'She is a all right. She is my little white bird. She is my little white dove.'

He winked and went upstairs. She and I sat there, and didn't say a word. When he came down he had a big bottle and a guitar. He poured some out of the bottle, but it was sweet Greek wine, and made me sick to my stomach. He started to sing. He had a tenor voice, not one of these little tenors like you hear on the radio, but a big tenor, and on the high notes he would put in a sob like on a Caruso record. But I couldn't listen to him now. I was feeling worse by the minute.

He saw my face and took me outside. 'Out in a air, you feel better.'

''S all right. I'll be all right.'

'Sit down. Keep quiet.'

'Go ahead in. I just ate too much lunch. I'll be all right.'

He went in, and I let everything come up. It was like hell the lunch, or the potatoes, or the wine. I wanted that woman so bad I couldn't even keep anything on my stomach.

Next morning the sign was blown down. About the middle of the night it had started to blow, and by morning it was a windstorm that took the sign with it.

'It's awful. Look at that.'

'Was a very big wind. I could no sleep. No sleep all night.'

'Big wind all right. But look at the sign.'

'Is busted.'

I kept tinkering with the sign, and he would come out and watch me. 'How did you get this sign anyway?'

'Was here when I buy the place. Why?'

'It's lousy all right. I wonder you do any business at all.'

I went to gas up a car, and left him to think that over. When I got back he was still blinking at it, where it was leaning against the front of the lunchroom. Three of the lights were busted. I plugged in the wire, and half of the others didn't light.

'Put in new lights, hang'm up, will be all right.'

'You're the boss.'

'What's a matter with it?'

'Well, it's out of date. Nobody has bulb signs any more. They got Neon signs. They show up better, and they don't burn as much juice. Then, what does it say? Twin Oaks, that's all. The Tavern part, it's not in lights. Well, Twin Oaks don't make me hungry. It don't make me want to stop and get something to eat. It's costing you money, that sign, only you don't know it.'

'Fix'm up, will be hokay.'

'Why don't you get a new sign?'

'I'm busy.'

But pretty soon he was back, with a piece of paper. He

had drew a new sign for himself, and colored it up with red, white, and blue crayon. It said Twin Oaks Tavern, and Eat, and Bar-B-Q, and Sanitary Rest Rooms, and N. Papadakis, Prop.

'Swell. That'll knock them for a loop.'

I fixed up the words, so they were spelled right, and he put some more curlycues on the letters.

'Nick, why do we hang up the old sign at all? Why don't you go to the city today and get this new sign made? It's a beauty, believe me it is. And it's important. A place is no better than its sign, is it?'

'I do it. By golly, I go.'

Los Angeles wasn't but twenty miles away, but he shined himself up like he was going to Paris, and right after lunch, he went. Soon as he was gone, I locked the front door. I picked up a plate that a guy had left, and went on back in the kitchen with it. She was there.

'Here's a plate that was out there.'

'Oh, thanks.'

I set it down. The fork was rattling like a tambourine.

'I was going to go, but I started some things cooking and I thought I better not.'

'I got plenty to do, myself.'

'You feeling better?'

'I'm all right.'

'Sometimes just some little thing will do it. Like a change of water, something like that.'

'Probably too much lunch.'

'What's that?'

Somebody was out front, rattling the door. 'Sounds like somebody trying to get in.'

'Is the door locked, Frank?'

'I must have locked it.'

She looked at me, and got pale. She went to the swinging

8

door, and peeped through. Then she went into the lunch-room, but in a minute she was back.

'They went away.'

'I don't know why I locked it.'

'I forgot to unlock it.'

She started for the lunchroom again. but I stopped her. 'Let's – leave it locked.'

'Nobody can get in if it's locked. I got some cooking to do. I'll wash up this plate.'

I took her in my arms and mashed my mouth up against hers . . . 'Bite me! Bite me!'

I bit her. I sunk my teeth into her lips so deep I could feel the blood spurt into my mouth. It was running down her neck when I carried her upstairs.

3

For two days after that I was dead, but the Greek was sore at me, so I got by all right. He was sore at me because I hadn't fixed the swing door that led from the lunchroom into the kitchen. She told him it swung back and hit her in the mouth. She had to tell him something. Her mouth was all swelled up where I had bit it. So he said it was my fault, that I hadn't fixed it. I stretched the spring, so it was weaker, and that fixed it.

But the real reason he was sore at me was over the sign. He had fallen for it so hard he was afraid I would say it was my idea, stead of his. It was such a hell of a sign they couldn't get it done for him that afternoon. It took them three days, and when it was ready I went in and got it and hung it up. It had on it all that he had drew on the paper, and a couple of other things besides. It had a Greek flag and an American flag, and hands shaking hands, and Satisfaction Guaranteed. It was all in red, white, and blue Neon letters, and I waited until dark to turn on the juice. When I snapped the switch, it lit up like a Christmas tree.

'Well, I've seen many a sign in my time, but never one like that. I got to hand it to you, Nick.'

'By golly. By golly.'

We shook hands. We were friends again.

*

Next day I was alone with her for a minute, and swung my fist up against her leg so hard it nearly knocked her over.

'How do you get that way?' She was snarling like a cougar. I liked her like that.

'How are you, Cora?'

'Lousy.'

From then on, I began to smell her again.

One day the Greek heard there was a guy up the road undercutting him on gas. He jumped in the car to go see about it. I was in my room when he drove off, and I turned around to dive down in the kitchen. But she was already there, standing in the door.

I went over and looked at her mouth. It was the first chance I had had to see how it was. The swelling was all gone, but you could still see the tooth marks, little blue creases on both lips. I touched them with my fingers. They were soft and damp. I kissed them, but not hard. They were little soft kisses. I had never thought about them before. She stayed until the Greek came back, about an hour. We didn't do anything. We just lay on the bed. She kept rumpling my hair, and looking up at the ceiling, like she was thinking.

'You like blueberry pie?'

'I don't know. Yeah. I guess so.'

'I'll make you some.'

'Look out, Frank. You'll break a spring leaf.'

'To hell with the spring leaf.'

We were crashing into a little eucalyptus grove beside the road. The Greek had sent us down to the market to take back some T-bone steaks he said were lousy, and on the way back it had got dark. I slammed the car in there, and it bucked and bounced, but when I was in among the trees I stopped. Her arms were around me before I even cut the lights. We

11

did plenty. After a while we just sat there. 'I can't go on like this, Frank.'

'Me neither.'

'I can't stand it. And I've got to get drunk with you, Frank. You know what I mean? Drunk.'

'I know.'

'And I hate that Greek.'

'Why did you marry him? You never did tell me that.'

'I haven't told you anything.'

'We haven't wasted any time on talk.'

'I was working in a hash house. You spend two years in a Los Angeles hash house and you'll take the first guy that's got a gold watch.'

'When did you leave Iowa?'

'Three years ago. I won a beauty contest. I won a high school beauty contest, in Des Moines. That's where I lived. The prize was a trip to Hollywood. I got off the Chief with fifteen guys taking my picture, and two weeks later I was in the hash house.'

'Didn't you go back?'

'I wouldn't give them the satisfaction.'

'Did you get in movies?'

'They gave me a test. It was all right in the face. But they talk, now. The pictures, I mean. And when I began to talk, up there on the screen, they knew me for what I was, and so did I. A cheap Des Moines trollop, that had as much chance in pictures as a monkey has. Not as much. A monkey, anyway, can make you laugh. All I did was make you sick.'

'And then?'

'Then two years of guys pinching your leg and leaving nickel tips and asking how about a little party tonight. I went on some of them parties, Frank.'

'And then?'

'You know what I mean about them parties?'

'I know.'

'Then he came along. I took him, and so help me, I meant to stick by him. But I can't stand it any more. God, do I look like a little white bird?'

'To me, you look more like a hell cat.'

'You know, don't you. That's one thing about you. I don't have to fool you all the time. And you're clean. You're not greasy. Frank, do you have any idea what that means? You're not greasy.'

'I can kind of imagine.'

'I don't think so. No man can know what that means to a woman. To have to be around somebody that's greasy and makes you sick at the stomach when he touches you. I'm not really such a hell cat, Frank. I just can't stand it any more.'

'What are you trying to do? Kid me?'

'Oh, all right. I'm a hell cat, then. But I don't think I would be so bad. With somebody that wasn't greasy.'

'Cora, how about you and me going away?'

'I've thought about it. I've thought about it a lot.'

'We'll ditch this Greek and blow. Just blow.'

'Where to?'

'Anywhere. What do we care?'

'Anywhere. Anywhere. You know where that is?'

'All over. Anywhere we choose.'

'No it's not. It's the hash house.'

'I'm not talking about the hash house. I'm talking about the road. It's fun, Cora. And nobody knows it better than I do. I know every twist and turn it's got. And I know how to work it, too. Isn't that what we want? Just to be a pair of tramps, like we really are?'

'You were a fine tramp. You didn't even have socks.'

'You liked me.'

'I loved you. I would love you without even a shirt. I would love you specially without a shirt, so I could feel how nice and hard your shoulders are.'

'Socking railroad detectives developed the muscles.'

'And you're hard all over. Big and tall and hard. And your hair is light. You're not a little soft greasy guy with black kinky hair that he puts bay rum on every night.'

'That must be a nice smell.'

'But it won't do, Frank. That road, it don't lead anywhere but to the hash house. The hash house for me, and some job like it for you. A lousy parking lot job, where you wear a smock. I'd cry if I saw you in a smock, Frank.'

'Well?'

She sat there a long time, twisting my hand in both of hers. 'Frank, do you love me?'

'Yes.'

'Do you love me so much that not anything matters?'

'Yes.'

'There's one way.'

'Did you say you weren't really a hell cat?'

'I said it, and I mean it. I'm not what you think I am, Frank. I want to work and be something, that's all. But you can't do it without love. Do you know that, Frank? Anyway, a woman can't. Well, I've made one mistake. And I've got to be a hell cat, just once, to fix it. But I'm not really a hell cat, Frank.'

'They hang you for that.'

'Not if you do it right. You're smart, Frank. I never fooled you for a minute. You'll think of a way. Plenty of them have. Don't worry. I'm not the first woman that had to turn hell cat to get out of a mess.'

'He never did anything to me. He's all right.'

'The hell he's all right. He stinks, I tell you. He's greasy and he stinks. And do you think I'm going to let you wear a smock, with Service Auto Parts printed on the back, Thank-U Call Again, while he has four suits and a dozen silk shirts? Isn't that business half mine? Don't I cook? Don't I cook good? Don't you do your part?'

'You talk like it was all right.'

'Who's going to know if it's all right or not, but you and me?'

'You and me.'

'That's it, Frank. That's all that matters, isn't it? Not you and me and the road, or anything else but you and me.'

'You must be a hell cat, though. You couldn't make me feel like this if you weren't.'

'That's what we're going to do. Kiss me, Frank. On the mouth.'

I kissed her. Her eyes were shining up at me like two blue stars. It was like being in church.

4

'Got any hot water?'

'What's the matter with the bathroom?'

'Nick's in there.'

'Oh. I'll give you some out of the kettle. He likes the whole heater full for his bath.'

We played it just like we would tell it. It was about ten o'clock at night, and we had closed up, and the Greek was in the bathroom, putting on his Saturday night wash. I was to take the water up to my room, get ready to shave, and then remember I had left the car out. I was to go outside, and stand by to give her one on the horn if somebody came. She was to wait till she heard him in the tub, go in for a towel, and clip him from behind with a blackjack I had made for her out of a sugar bag with ball bearings wadded down in the end. At first, I was to do it, but we figured he wouldn't pay any attention to her if she went in there, where if I said I was after my razor, he might get out of the tub or something and help me look. Then she was to hold him under until he drowned. Then she was to leave the water running a little bit, and step out the window to the porch roof, and come down the stepladder I had put there, to the ground. She was to hand me the blackjack, and go back to the kitchen. I was to put the ball bearings back in the box, throw the bag away, put the car in, and go up to my room and start to shave. She would wait till the water began dripping down in the kitchen, and call me. We would break the door down, find him, and call the doctor. In the end, we figured it would look like he had slipped in the tub, knocked himself out, and then drowned. I got the idea from a piece in the paper where a guy had said that most accidents happen right in people's own bathtubs.

'Be careful of it. It's hot.'

'Thanks.'

It was in a saucepan, and I took it up in my room and set it on the bureau, and laid my shaving stuff out. I went down and out to the car, and took a seat in it so I could see the road and the bathroom window, both. The Greek was singing. It came to me I better take note what the song was. It was Mother Machree. He sang it once, and then sang it over again. I looked in the kitchen. She was still there.

A truck and a trailer swung around the bend. I fingered the horn. Sometimes those truckmen stopped for something to eat, and they were the kind that would beat on the door till you opened up. But they went on. A couple more cars went by. They didn't stop. I looked in the kitchen again, and she wasn't there. A light went on in the bedroom.

Then, all of a sudden, I saw something move, back by the porch. I almost hit the horn, but then I saw it was a cat. It was just a grey cat, but it shook me up. A cat was the last thing I wanted to see then. I couldn't see it for a minute, and then there it was again, smelling around the stepladder. I didn't want to blow the horn, because it wasn't anything but a cat, but I didn't want it around that stepladder. I got out of the car, went back there, and shooed it away.

I got halfway back to the car, when it came back, and started up the ladder. I shooed it away again, and ran it clear back to the shacks. I started back to the car, and then stood there for a little bit, looking to see if it was coming back. A state cop came around the bend. He saw me standing there, cut his motor, and came wheeling in, before I could move. When he stopped he was between me and the car. I couldn't blow the horn.

'Taking it easy?'

'Just came out to put the car away.'

'That your car?'

'Belongs to this guy I work for.'

'OK. Just checking up.'

He looked around, and then he saw something. 'I'll be damned. Look at that.'

'Look at what?'

'Goddam cat, going up that stepladder.'

'Ha.'

'I love a cat. They're always up to something.'

He pulled on his gloves, took a look at the night, kicked his pedal a couple of times, and went. Soon as he was out of sight I dove for the horn. I was too late. There was a flash of fire from the porch, and every light in the place went out. Inside, Cora was screaming with an awful sound in her voice. 'Frank! Frank! Something has happened!'

I ran in the kitchen, but it was black dark in there and I didn't have any matches in my pocket, and I had to feel my way. We met on the stairs, she going down, and me going up. She screamed again.

'Keep quiet, for God's sake keep quiet! Did you do it?'

'Yes, but the lights went out, and I haven't held him under yet!'

'We got to bring him to! There was a state cop out there, and he saw that stepladder!'

'Phone for the doctor!'

'You phone, and I'll get him out of there!'

She went down, and I kept on up. I went in the bathroom, and over to the tub. He was laying there in the water, but his head wasn't under. I tried to lift him. I had a hell of a time.

He was slippery with soap, and I had to stand in the water before I could raise him at all. All the time I could hear her down there, talking to the operator. They didn't give her a doctor. They gave her the police.

I got him up, and laid him over the edge of the tub, and then got out myself, and dragged him in the bedroom and laid him on the bed. She came up, then, and we found matches, and got a candle lit. Then we went to work on him. I packed his head in wet towels, while she rubbed his wrists and feet.

'They're sending an ambulance.'

'All right. Did he see you do it?'

'I don't know.'

'Were you behind him?'

'I think so. But then the lights went out, and I don't know what happened. What did you do to the lights?'

'Nothing. The fuse popped.'

'Frank. He'd better not come to.'

'He's got to come to. If he dies, we're sunk. I tell you, that cop saw the stepladder. If he dies, then they'll know. If he dies, they've got us.'

'But suppose he saw me? What's he going to say when he comes to?'

'Maybe he didn't. We just got to sell him a story, that's all. You were in here, and the lights popped, and you heard him slip and fall, and he didn't answer when you spoke to him. Then you called me, that's all. No matter what he says, you got to stick to it. If he saw anything, it was just his imagination, that's all.'

'Why don't they hurry with that ambulance?'

'It'll be here.'

Soon as the ambulance came, they put him on a stretcher and shoved him in. She rode with him. I followed along in the car. Halfway to Glendale, a state cop picked us up and rode on ahead. They went seventy miles an hour, and I couldn't keep up. They were lifting him out when I got to the hospital, and the state cop was bossing the job. When he saw me he gave a start and stared at me. It was the same cop.

They took him in, put him on a table, and wheeled him in an operating room. Cora and myself sat out in the hall. Pretty soon a nurse came and sat down with us. Then the cop came, and he had a sergeant with him. They kept looking at me. Cora was telling the nurse how it happened. 'I was in there, in the bathroom I mean, getting a towel, and then the lights went out just like somebody had shot a gun off. Oh my, they made a terrible noise. I heard him fall. He had been standing up, getting ready to turn on the shower. I spoke to him, and he didn't say anything, and it was all dark, and I couldn't see anything, and I didn't know what had happened. I mean I thought he had been electrocuted or something. So then Frank heard me screaming, and he came, and got him out, and then I called up for the ambulance, and I don't know what I would have done if they hadn't come quick like they did.'

'They always hurry on a late call.'

'I'm so afraid he's hurt bad.'

'I don't think so. They're taking X-Rays in there now. They can always tell from X-Rays. But I don't think he's hurt bad.'

'Oh my, I hope not.'

The cops never said a word. They just sat there and looked at us.

They wheeled him out, and his head was covered with bandages. They put him on an elevator, and Cora, and me, and the nurse, and the cops all got on, and they took him up and put him in a room. We all went in there. There weren't enough chairs and while they were putting him to bed the nurse went and got some extra ones. We all sat down. Somebody said something, and the nurse made them keep quiet. A doctor came and took a look, and went out. We sat there a hell of a while. Then the nurse went over and looked at him.

'I think he's coming to now.'

Cora looked at me, and I looked away quick. The cops leaned forward, to hear what he said. He opened his eyes.

'You feel better now?'

He didn't say anything and neither did anybody else. It was so still I could hear my heart pounding in my ears. 'Don't you know your wife? Here she is. Aren't you ashamed of yourself, falling in the bathtub like a little boy, just because the lights went out. Your wife is mad at you. Aren't you going to speak to her?'

He strained to say something, but couldn't say it. The nurse went over and fanned him. Cora took hold of his hand and patted it. He lay back for a few minutes, with his eyes closed, and then his mouth began to move again and he looked at the nurse.

'Was a all go dark.'

When the nurse said he had to be quiet, I took Cora down, and put her in the car. We no sooner started out than the cop was back there, following us on his motorcycle.

'He suspicions us, Frank.'

'It's the same one. He knew there was something wrong, soon as he saw me standing there, keeping watch. He still thinks so.'

'What are we going to do?'

'I don't know. It all depends on that stepladder, whether he tumbles what it's there for. What did you do with that slungshot?'

'I still got it here, in the pocket of my dress.'

'God Almighty, if they had arrested you back there, and searched you, we'd have been sunk.'

I gave her my knife, made her cut the string off the bag,

and take the bearings out. Then I made her climb back, raise the back seat, and put the bag under it. It would look like a rag, like anybody keeps with the tools.

'You stay back there, now, and keep an eye on that cop. I'm going to snap these bearings into the bushes one at a time, and you've got to watch if he notices anything.'

She watched, and I drove with my left hand, and leaned my right hand on the wheel. I let go. I shot it like a marble, out the window and across the road.

'Did he turn his head?'

'No.'

I let the rest go, one every couple of minutes. He never noticed it.

We got out to the place, and it was still dark. I hadn't had time to find the fuses, let alone put a new one in. When I pulled in, the cop went past, and was there ahead of me. 'I'm taking a look at that fuse box, buddy.'

'Sure. I'm taking a look myself.'

We all three went back there, and he snapped on a flashlight. Right away, he gave a funny grunt and stooped down. There was the cat, laying on its back with all four feet in the air.

'Ain't that a shame? Killed her deader than hell.'

He shot the flashlight up under the porch roof, and along the stepladder. 'That's it, all right. Remember? We were looking at her. She stepped off the ladder on to your fuse box, and it killed her deader than hell.'

'That's it all right. You were hardly gone when it happened. Went off like a pistol shot. I hadn't even had time to move the car.'

'They caught me down the road.'

'You were hardly out of sight.'

'Stepped right off the ladder on to the fuse box. Well, that's the way it goes. Them poor dumb things, they can't get it through their head about electricity, can they? No sir, it's too much for them.'

'Tough, all right.'

'That's what it is, it's tough. Killed her deader than hell. Pretty cat, too. Remember, how she looked when she was creeping up that ladder? I never seen a cuter cat than she was.'

'And pretty color.'

'And killed her deader than hell. Well, I'll be going along. I guess that straightens us out. Had to check up, you know.'

'That's right.'

'So long. So long, Miss.'

'So long.'

5

We didn't do anything about the cat, the fuse box, or anything else. We crept into bed, and she cracked up. She cried, and then got a chill so she was trembling all over, and it was a couple of hours before I could get her quiet. She lay in my arms a while, then, and we began to talk.

'Never again, Frank.'

'That's right. Never again.'

'We must have been crazy. Just plain crazy.'

'Just our dumb luck that pulled us through.'

'It was my fault.'

'Mine too.'

'No, it was my fault. I was the one that thought it up. You didn't want to. Next time I'll listen to you, Frank. You're smart. You're not dumb like I am.'

'Except there won't be any next time.'

'That's right. Never again.'

'Even if we had gone through with it they would have guessed it. They *always* guess it. They guess it anyway, just from habit. Because look how quick that cop knew something was wrong. That's what makes my blood run cold. Soon as he saw me standing there he knew it. If he could tumble to it all that easy, how much chance would we have had if the Greek had died?'

'I guess I'm not really a hell cat, Frank.'

'I'm telling you.'

'If I was, I wouldn't have got scared so easy. I was *so* scared, Frank.'

'I was scared plenty, myself.'

'You know what I wanted when the lights went out? Just you, Frank. I wasn't any hell cat at all, then. I was just a little girl, afraid of the dark.'

'I was there, wasn't I?'

'I loved you for it. If it hadn't been for you, I don't know what would have happened to us.'

'Pretty good, wasn't it? About how he slipped?'

'And he believed it.'

'Give me half a chance, I got it on the cops, every time. You got to have something to tell, that's it. You got to fill in all those places, and yet have it as near the truth as you can get it. I know them. I've tangled with them, plenty.'

'You fixed it. You're always going to fix it for me, aren't you, Frank?'

'You're the only one ever meant anything to me.'

'I guess I really don't want to be a hell cat.'

'You're my baby.'

'That's it, just your dumb baby. All right, Frank. I'll listen to you, from now on. You be the brains, and I'll work. I can work, Frank. And I work good. We'll get along.'

'Sure we will.'

'Now shall we go to sleep?'

'You think you can sleep all right?'

'It's the first time we ever slept together, Frank.'

'You like it?'

'It's grand, just grand.'

'Kiss me goodnight.'

'It's so sweet to be able to kiss you goodnight.'

Next morning, the telephone waked us up. She answered it, and when she came up her eyes were shining. 'Frank, guess what?'

'What?'

'His skull is fractured.'

'Bad?'

'No, but they're keeping him there. They want him there for a week, maybe. We can sleep together again, tonight.'

'Come here.'

'Not now. We've got to get up. We've got to open the place up.'

'Come here, before I sock you.'

'You nut.'

It was a happy week, all right. In the afternoon, she would drive in to the hospital, but the rest of the time we were together. We gave him a break, too. We kept the place open all the time, and went after the business, and got it. Of course it helped, that day when a hundred Sunday school kids showed up in three buses, and wanted a bunch of stuff to take out in the woods with them, but even without that we would have made plenty. The cash register didn't know anything to tell on us, believe me it didn't.

Then one day, stead of her going in alone, we both went in, and after she came out of the hospital, we cut for the beach. They gave her a yellow suit and a red cap, and when she came out I didn't know her at first. She looked like a little girl. It was the first time I ever really saw how young she was. We played in the sand, and then we went way out and let the swells rock us. I like my head to the waves, she liked her feet. We lay there, face to face, and held hands under water. I looked up at the sky. It was all you could see. I thought about God.

'Frank.'

'Yes?'

'He's coming home tomorrow. You know what that means?'

'I know.'

'I got to sleep with him, stead of you.'

'You would, except that when he gets here we're going to be gone.'

'I was hoping you'd say that.'

'Just you and me and the road, Cora.'

'Just you and me and the road.'

'Just a couple of tramps.'

'Just a couple of gypsies, but we'll be together.'

'That's it. We'll be together.'

Next morning, we packed up. Anyway, she packed. I had bought a suit, and I put that on, and it seemed to be about all. She put her things in a hatbox. When she got done with it, she handed it to me. 'Put that in the car, will you?'

'The car?'

'Aren't we taking the car?'

'Not unless you want to spend the first night in jail, we're not. Stealing a man's wife, that's nothing, but stealing his car, that's larceny.'

'Oh.'

We started out. It was two miles to the bus stop, and we had to hike it. Every time a car went by, we would stand there with our hand stuck out, like a cigar store Indian, but none of them stopped. A man alone can get a ride, and a woman alone, if she's fool enough to take it, but a man and a woman together don't have much luck. After about twenty had gone by, she stopped. We had gone about a quarter of a mile.

'Frank, I can't.'

'What's the matter?'

'This is it.'

'This is what?'

'The road.'

'You're crazy. You're tired, that's all. Look. You wait here, and I'll get somebody down the road to drive us in to the city. That's what we ought to done anyhow. Then we'll be all right.'

'No, it's not that. I'm not tired. I can't, that's all. At all.'

'Don't you want to be with me, Cora?'

'You know I do.'

'We can't go back, you know. We can't start up again, like it was before. You know that. You've got to come.'

'I told you I wasn't really a bum, Frank. I don't feel like no gypsy. I don't feel like nothing, only ashamed, that I'm out here asking for a ride.'

'I told you. We're getting a car in to the city.'

'And then what?'

'Then we're there. Then we get going.'

'No we don't. We spend one night in a hotel, and then we start looking for a job. And living in a dump.'

'Isn't that a dump? What you just left?'

'It's different.'

'Cora, you going to let it get your goat?'

'It's got it, Frank. I can't go on. Goodbye.'

'Will you listen to me a minute?'

'Goodbye, Frank. I'm going back.'

She kept tugging at the hatbox. I tried to hold on to it, anyway to carry it back for her, but she got it. She started back with it. She had looked nice when she started out, with a little blue suit and blue hat, but now she looked all battered, and her shoes were dusty, and she couldn't even walk right, from crying. All of a sudden, I found out I was crying too.

caught a ride to San Bernardino. It's a railroad town, and I was going to hop a freight east. But I didn't do it. I ran into a guy in a poolroom, and began playing him one ball in the side. He was the greatest job in the way of a sucker that God ever turned out, because he had a friend that could really play. The only trouble with him was, he couldn't play good enough. I hung around with the pair of them a couple of weeks, and took $250 off them, all they had, and then I had to beat it out of town quick.

I caught a truck for Mexicali, and then I got to thinking about my $250, and how with that much money we could go to the beach and sell hot dogs or something until we got a stake to take a crack at something bigger. So I dropped off, and caught a ride back to Glendale. I began hanging around the market where they bought their stuff, hoping I would bump into her. I even called her up a couple of times, but the Greek answered and I had to make out it was a wrong number. In between walking around the market, I hung around a poolroom, about a block down the street, One day a guy was practicing shots alone on one of the tables. You could tell he was new at it from the way he held his cue. I began practicing shots on the next table. I figured if $250 was enough for a hot dog stand, $350 would leave us sitting pretty.

'How you say to a little one ball in the side?'

'I never played that game much.'

'Nothing to it. Just the one ball in the side pocket.'

'Anyhow, you look too good for me.'

'Me? I'm just a punk.'

'Oh well. If it's just a friendly game.'

We started to play, and I let him take three or four, just to feel good. I kept shaking my head, like I couldn't understand it.

'Too good for you, hey. Well, that's a joke. But I swear, I'm really better than this. I can't seem to get going. How you say we put $1 on it, just to make it lively?'

'Oh well. I can't lose much at a dollar.'

We made it $1 a game, and I let him take four or five, maybe more. I shot like I was pretty nervous, and in between shots I would wipe off the palm of my hand with a handkerchief, like I must be sweating.

'Well, it looks like I'm not doing so good. How about making it $5, so I can get my money back, and then we'll go have a drink?'

'Oh well. It's just a friendly game, and I don't want your money. Sure. We'll make it $5, and then we'll quit.'

I let him take four or five more, and from the way I was acting, you would have thought I had heart failure and a couple more things besides. I was plenty blue around the gills.

'Look. I got sense enough to know when I'm out of my class all right, but let's make it $25, so I can break even, and then we'll go have that drink.'

'That's pretty high for me.'

'What the hell? You're playing on my money, aren't you?'

'Oh well. All right. Make it $25.'

Then was when I really started to shoot. I made shots that Hoppe couldn't make. I banked them in from three cushions, I made billiard shots, I had my english working so the ball just floated around the table, I even called a jump shot and made it. He never made a shot that Blind Tom the Sightless Piano Player couldn't have made. He miscued, he got himself all tangled up on position, he scratched, he put the one ball in the wrong pocket, he never even called a bank shot. And when I walked out of there, he had my $250 and a $3 watch that I had bought to keep track of when Cora might be driving in to the market. Oh, I was good all right. The only trouble was I wasn't quite good enough.

'Hey, Frank!'

It was the Greek, running across the street at me before I had really got out the door.

'Well Frank, you old son a gun, where you been, put her there, why you run away from me just a time I hurt my head I need you most?'

We shook hands. He still had a bandage around his head and a funny look in his eyes, but he was all dressed up in a new suit, and had a black hat cocked over on the side of his head, and a purple necktie, and brown shoes, and his gold watch chain looped across his vest, and a big cigar in his hand.

'Well, Nick! How you feeling, boy?'

'Me, I feel fine, couldn't feel better if was right out a the can, but why you run out on me? I sore as hell at you, you old son a gun.'

'Well, you know me, Nick. I stay put a while, and then I got to ramble.'

'You pick one hell of a time to ramble. What you do, hey? Come on, you don't do nothing, you old son a gun, I know you, come on over while I buy'm steaks I tell you all about it.'

'You alone?'

'Don't talk so dumb, who the hell you think keep a place open now you run out on me, hey? Sure I'm alone. Me a

Cora never get to go out together now, one go, other have to stay.'

'Well then, let's walk over.'

It took him an hour to buy the steaks, he was so busy telling me how his skull was fractured, how the docs never saw a fracture like it, what a hell of a time he's had with his help, how he's had two guys since I left and he fired one the day after he hired him, and the other one skipped after three days and took the inside of the cash register with him, and how he'd give anything to have me back.

'Frank, I tell you what. We go to Santa Barbara tomorrow, me a Cora. Hell boy, we got to step out a little, hey? We go see a fiesta there, and you come with us. You like that, Frank? You come with us, we talk about you come back a work for me. You like a fiesta a Santa Barbara?'

'Well, I hear it's good.'

'Is a girls, is a music, is a dance in streets, is swell. Come on, Frank, what you say?'

'Well, I don't know.'

'Cora be sore as hell at me if I see you and no bring you out. Maybe she treat you snotty, but she think you fine fellow, Frank. Come on, we all three go. We have a hell of a time.'

'OK. If she's willing, it's a go.'

There were eight or ten people in the lunchroom when we got there, and she was back in the kitchen, washing dishes as fast as she could, to get enough plates to serve them.

'Hey. Hey Cora, look. Look who I bring.'

'Well for heaven's sake. Where did he come from?'

'I see'm today a Glendale. He go to Santa Barbara with us.'

'Hello, Cora. How you been?'

'You're quite a stranger around here.'

She wiped her hands quick, and shook hands, but her hand was soapy. She went out front with an order, and me and the Greek sat down. He generally helped her with the orders, but he was all hot to show me something, and he let her do it all alone. It was a big scrapbook, and in the front of it he had pasted his naturalization certificate, and then his wedding certificate, and then his license to do business in Los Angeles County, and then a picture of himself in the Greek Army, and then a picture of him and Cora the day they got married, and then all the clippings about his accident. Those clippings in the regular papers, if you ask me, were more about the cat than they were about him, but anyway they had his name in them, and how he had been brought to the Glendale Hospital, and was expected to recover. The one in the Los Angeles Greek paper, though, was more about him than about the cat, and had a picture of him in it, in the dress suit he had when he was a waiter, and the story of his life. Then came the X-Rays. There were about a half dozen of them, because they took a new picture every day to see how he was getting along. How he had them fixed up was to paste two pages together, along the edges, and then cut out a square place in the middle, where the X-Ray was slipped in so you could hold it up to the light and look through it. After the X-Rays came the receipted hospital bills, the receipted doctors' bills, and the receipted nurses' bills. That rap on the conk cost him $322, believe it or not.

'Is a nice, hey?'

'Swell. It's all there, right on the line.'

'Of course, is a not done yet. I fix'm up red, a white, a blue, fix'm up fine. Look.'

He showed me where he had put the fancy stuff on a couple of the pages. He had inked in the curlycues, and then colored it with red, white, and blue. Over the naturalization certificate, he had a couple of American flags, and an eagle, and over the Greek Army picture he had crossed Greek flags, and another eagle, and over his wedding certificate he had a couple of turtle doves on a twig. He hadn't figured out yet what to put over the other stuff, but I said over the clippings he could put a cat with red, white, and blue fire coming out of its tail, and he thought that was pretty good. He didn't get it, though, when I said he could have a buzzard over the Los Angeles County license, holding a couple of auctioneer's flags that said Sale Today, and it didn't look like it would really be worth while to try to explain it to him. But I got it, at last, why he was all dressed up, and not carrying out the chow like he used to, and acted so important. This Greek had had a fracture of the skull, and a thing like that don't happen to a dumb cluck like him every day. He was like a wop that opens a drug store. Soon as he gets that thing that says Pharmacist, with a red seal on it, a wop puts on a grey suit, with black edges on the vest, and is so important he can't even take time to mix the pills, and wouldn't even touch a chocolate ice-cream soda. This Greek was all dressed up for the same reason. A big thing had happened in his life.

It was pretty near supper time when I got her alone. He went up to wash, and the two of us were left in the kitchen.

'You been thinking about me, Cora?'

'Sure. I wouldn't forget you all that quick.'

'I thought about you a lot. How are you?'

'Me? I'm all right.'

'I called you up a couple of times, but he answered and I was afraid to talk to him. I made some money.'

'Well, gee, I'm glad you're getting along good.'

'I made it, but then I lost it. I thought we could use it to get started with, but then I lost it.'

'I declare, I don't know where the money goes.'

'You sure you think about me, Cora?'

'Sure I do.'

'You don't act like it.'

'Seems to me I'm acting all right.'

'Have you got a kiss for me?'

'We'll be having supper pretty soon. You better get ready, if you've got any washing to do.'

That's the way it went. That's the way it went all evening. The Greek got out some of his sweet wine, and sang a bunch of songs, and we sat around, and so far as she was concerned, I might just as well have been just a guy that used to work there, only she couldn't quite remember his name. It was the worst flop of a home-coming you ever saw in your life.

When it came to go to bed, I let them go up, and then I went outside to try and figure out whether to stay there and see if I couldn't get going with her again, or blow and try to forget her. I walked quite a way off, and I don't know how long it was, or how far away I was, but after a while I could hear a row going on in the place. I went back, and when I got close I could hear some of what they were saying. She was yelling like hell and saying I had to leave. He was mumbling something, probably that he wanted me to stay and go back to work. He was trying to shut her up, but I could tell she was yelling so I would hear it. If I had been in my room, where she thought I was, I could have heard it plain enough, and even where I was I could hear plenty.

Then all of a sudden it stopped. I slipped in the kitchen, and stood there listening. But I couldn't hear anything, because I was all shook up, and all I could get was the sound of my own heart, going bump-bump, bump-bump, bump-bump, like that. I thought that was a funny way for my heart to sound, and then all of a sudden I knew there was two hearts in that kitchen, and that was why it sounded so funny.

I snapped on the light.

She was standing there, in a red kimono, as pale as milk, staring at me, with a long thin knife in her hand. I reached out and took it away from her. When she spoke, it was in a whisper that sounded like a snake licking its tongue in and out.

'Why did you have to come back?'

'I had to, that's all.'

'No you didn't. I could have gone through with it. I was getting so I could forget you. And now you have to come back. God damn you, you have to come back!'

'Go through with what?'

'What he's making that scrapbook for. *It's to show to his children!* And now he wants one. He wants one right away.'

'Well, why didn't you come with me?'

'Come with you for what? To sleep in box cars? Why would I come with you? Tell me that.'

I couldn't say anything. I thought about my $250, but what good was it telling her that I had some money yesterday, but today I lost it playing one ball in the side?

'You're no good. I know that. You're just no good. Then why don't you go away and let me alone instead of coming back here again? Why don't you leave me be?'

'Listen. Stall him on this kid stuff just a little while. Stall him, and we'll see if we can't figure something out. I'm not much good, but I love you, Cora. I swear it.'

'You swear it, and what do you do? He's taking me to Santa Barbara, so I'll say I'll have the child, and you – you're going right along with us. You're going to stay at the same hotel with us! You're going right along in the car. You're—'

She stopped, and we stood there looking at each other. The three of us in the car, we knew what that meant. Little by little we were nearer, until we were touching.

'Oh, my God, Frank, isn't there any other way out for us than that?'

'Well. You were going to stick a knife in him just now.'

'No. That was for me, Frank. Not him.'

'Cora, it's in the cards. We've tried every other way out.'

'I can't have no greasy Greek child, Frank. I can't, that's all. The only one I can have a child by is you. I wish you were some good. You're smart, but you're no good.'

'I'm no good, but I love you.'
'Yes, and I love you.'
'Stall him. Just this one night.'
'All right, Frank. Just this one night.'

7

'There's a long, long trail a-winding
Into the land of my dreams,
Where the nightingale is singing
And the white moon beams.

'There's a long, long night of waiting
Until my dreams all come true,
Till the day when I'll be going down
That long, long trail with you.'

'Feeling good, ain't they?'

'Too good to suit me.'

'So you don't let them get hold of that wheel, Miss. They'll
be all right.'

'I hope so. I've got no business out with a pair of drunks,
I know that. But what could I do? I told them I wouldn't go
with them, but then they started to go off by themselves.'

'They'd break their necks.'

'That's it. So I drove myself. It was all *I* knew to do.'

'It keeps you guessing, sometimes, to know what to do.
One sixty for the gas. Is the oil OK?'

'I think so.'

'Thanks, Miss. Goodnight.'

She got in, and took the wheel again, and me and the

Greek kept on singing, and we went on. It was all part of the play. I had to be drunk, because that other time had cured me of this idea we could pull a perfect murder. This was going to be such a lousy murder it wouldn't even be a murder. It was going to be just a regular road accident, with guys drunk, and booze in the car, and all the rest of it. Of course, when I started to put it down, the Greek had to have some too, so he was just like I wanted him. We stopped for gas so there would be a witness that she was sober, and didn't want to be with us anyhow, because she was driving, and it wouldn't do for her to be drunk. Before that, we had had a piece of luck. Just before we closed up, about nine o'clock, a guy stopped by for something to eat, and stood there in the road and watched us when we shoved off. He saw the whole show. He saw me try to start, and stall a couple of times. He heard the argument between me and Cora, about how I was too drunk to drive. He saw her get out, and heard her say she wasn't going. He saw me try to drive off, just me and the Greek. He saw her when she made us get out, and switched the seats, so I was behind, and the Greek up front, and then he saw her take the wheel and do the driving herself. His name was Jeff Parker and he raised rabbits at Encino. Cora got his card when she said she might try rabbits in the lunchroom, to see how they'd go. We knew right where to find him, whenever we'd need him.

Me and the Greek sang Mother Machree, and Smile, Smile, Smile, and Down by the Old Mill Stream, and pretty soon we came to this sign that said To Malibu Beach. She turned off there. By rights, she ought to have kept on like she was going. There's two main roads that lead up the coast. One, about ten miles inland, was the one we were on. The other, right alongside the ocean, was off to our left. At Ventura they meet, and follow the sea right on up to Santa Barbara, San Francisco, and wherever you're going. But the idea was, she had never seen Malibu Beach, where the movie stars live, and she wanted to cut over on this road to the ocean, so she could drop down a couple of miles and look at it, and then turn around and keep right on up to Santa Barbara. The real idea was that this connection is about the worst piece of road in Los Angeles County, and an accident there wouldn't surprise anybody, not even a cop. It's dark, and has no traffic on it hardly, and no houses or anything, and suited us for what we had to do.

The Greek never noticed anything for a while. We passed a little summer colony that they call Malibu Lake up in the hills, and there was a dance going on at the clubhouse, with couples out on the lake in canoes. I yelled at them. So did the Greek. 'Give a one f'me.' It didn't make much difference, but it was one more mark on our trail, if somebody took the trouble to find it.

We started up the first long up-grade, into the mountains. There were three miles of it. I had told her how to run it. Most of the time she was in second. That was partly because there were sharp curves every fifty feet, and the car would lose speed so quick going around them that she would have to shift up to second to keep going. But it was partly because the motor had to heat. Everything had to check up. We had to have plenty to tell.

And then, when he looked out and saw how dark it was, and what a hell of a looking country those mountains were, with no light, or house, or filling station, or anything else in sight, the Greek came to life and started an argument.

'Hold on, hold on. Turn around. By golly, we off the road.'

'No we're not. I know where I am. It takes us to Malibu Beach. Don't you remember? I told you I wanted to see it.'

'You go slow.'

'I'm going slow.'

'You go plenty slow. Maybe all get killed.'

*

We got to the top and started into the down-grade. She cut the motor. They heat fast for a few minutes, when the fan stops. Down at the bottom she started the motor again. I looked at the temp gauge. It was 200. She started into the next up-grade and the temp gauge kept climbing.

'Yes sir, yes sir.'

It was our signal. It was one of those dumb things a guy can say any time, and nobody will pay any attention to it. She pulled off to one side. Under us was a drop so deep you couldn't see the bottom of it. It must have been 500 feet.

'I think I'll let it cool off a bit.'

'By golly, you bet. Frank, look a that. Look what it says.'

'Whassit say?'

'Two hundred a five. Would be boiling in minute.'

'Letta boil.'

I picked up the wrench. I had it between my feet. But just then, way up the grade, I saw the lights of a car. I had to stall. I had to stall for a minute, until that car went by.

'C'me on, Nick. Sing's a song.'

He looked out on those bad lands, but he didn't seem to feel like singing. Then he opened the door and got out. We could hear him back there, sick. That was where he was when the car went by. I looked at the number to burn it in my brain. Then I burst out laughing. She looked back at me.

''S all right. Give them something to remember. Both guys alive when they went by.'

'Did you get the number?'

'2R–58–01.'

'2R–58–01. 2R–58–01. All right. I've got it too.'

'OK.'

He came around from behind, and looked like he felt better. 'You hear that?'

'Hear what?'

'When you laugh. Is a echo. Is a fine echo.'

He tossed off a high note. It wasn't any song, just a high

note, like on a Caruso record. He cut if off quick and listened. Sure enough, here it came back, clear as anything, and stopped, just like he had.

'Is a sound like me?'

'Jus' like you, kid. Jussa same ol' toot.'

'By golly. Is swell.'

He stood there for five minutes, tossing off high notes and listening to them come back. It was the first time he ever heard what his voice sounded like. He was as pleased as a gorilla that seen his face in the mirror. She kept looking at me. We had to get busy. I began to act sore. 'Wot th' hell? You think we got noth'n t' do but lis'n at you yod'l at y'self all night? C'me on, get in. Le's get going.'

'It's getting late, Nick,'

'Hokay, hokay.'

He got in, but shoved his face out to the window and let go one. I braced my feet, and while he still had his chin on the window sill I brought down the wrench. His head cracked, and I felt it crush. He crumpled up and curled on the seat like a cat on a sofa. It seemed a year before he was still. Then Cora, she gave a funny kind of gulp that ended in a moan. Because here came the echo of his voice. It took the high note, like he did, and swelled, and stopped, and waited.

8

We didn't say anything. She knew what to do. She climbed back, and I climbed front. I looked at the wrench under the dash light. It had a few drops of blood on it. I uncorked a bottle of wine, and poured it on there till the blood was gone. I poured so the wine went over him. Then I wiped the wrench on a dry part of his clothes, and passed it back to her. She put it under the seat. I poured more wine over where I had wiped the wrench, cracked the bottle against the door, and laid it on top of him. Then I started the car. The wine bottle gave a gurgle, where a little of it was running out the crack.

I went a little way, and then shifted up to second. I couldn't tip it down that 500-foot drop, where we were. We had to get down to it afterward, and besides, if it plunged that far, how would we be alive? I drove slow, in second, up to a place where the ravine came to a point, and it was only a 50-foot drop. When I got there, I drove over to the edge, put my foot on the brake, and fed with the hand throttle. As soon as the right front wheel went off, I stepped hard on the brake. It stalled. That was how I wanted it. The car had to be in gear, with the ignition on, but that dead motor would hold it for the rest of what we had to do.

We got out. We stepped on the road, not the shoulder, so there wouldn't be footprints. She handed me a rock, and a piece of 2x4 I had back there. I put the rock under the rear axle. It fitted, because I had picked one that would fit. I slipped the 2x4 over the rock and under the axle. I heaved down on it. The car tipped, but it hung there. I heaved again. It tipped a little more: I began to sweat. Here we were, with a dead man in the car, and suppose we couldn't tip it over?

I heaved again, but this time she was beside me. We both heaved. We heaved again. And then all of a sudden, there we were, sprawled down on the road, and the car was rolling over and over, down the gully, and banging so loud you could hear it a mile.

It stopped. The lights were still on, but it wasn't on fire. That was the big danger. With that ignition on, if the car burned up, why weren't we burned too? I snatched up the rock, and gave it a heave down the ravine. I picked up the 2x4, ran up the road with it a way, and slung it down, right in the roadway. It didn't bother me any. All over the road, wherever you go, are pieces of wood that have dropped off trucks, and they get all splintered up from cars running over them, and this was one of them. I had left it out all day, and it had tire marks on it, and the edges were all chewed up.

I ran back, picked her up, and slid down the ravine with her. Why I did that was on account of the tracks. My tracks, they didn't worry me any. I figured there would be plenty of men piling down there pretty soon, but those sharp heels of hers, they had to be pointed in the right direction, if anybody took the trouble to look.

I set her down. The car was hanging there, on two wheels, about halfway down the ravine. He was still in there, but now he was down on the floor. The wine bottle was wedged between him and the seat, and while we were looking it gave a gurgle. The top was all broken in, and both fenders were bent. I tried the doors. That was important, because I had to get in there, and be cut up with glass, while she went up on the road to get help. They opened all right.

I began to fool with her blouse, to bust the buttons, so she would look banged up. She was looking at me, and her eyes didn't look blue, they looked black. I could feel her breath coming fast. Then it stopped, and she leaned real close to me.

'Rip me! Rip me!'

I ripped her. I shoved my hand in her blouse and jerked. She was wide open, from her throat to her belly.

'You got that climbing out. You caught it in the door handle.'

My voice sounded queer, like it was coming out of a tin phonograph.

'And this you don't know how you got.'

I hauled off and hit her in the eye as hard as I could. She went down. She was right down there at my feet, her eyes shining, her breasts trembling, drawn up in tight points, and pointing right up at me. She was down there, and the breath was roaring in the back of my throat like I was some kind of a animal, and my tongue was all swelled up in my mouth, and blood pounding in it.

'Yes! Yes, Frank, yes!'

Next thing I knew, I was down there with her, and we were staring in each other's eyes, and locked in each other's arms, and straining to get closer. Hell could have opened for me then, and it wouldn't have made any difference. I had to have her, if I hung for it.

I had her.

9

We lay there a few minutes, then, like we were doped. It was so still that all you could hear was this gurgle from the inside of the car.

'What now, Frank?'

'Tough road ahead, Cora. You've got to be good, from now on. You sure you can go through it?'

'After that, I can go through anything.'

'They'll come at you, those cops. They'll try to break you down. You ready for them?'

'I think so.'

'Maybe they'll pin something on you. I don't think they can, with those witnesses we got. But maybe they do it. Maybe they pin it on you for manslaughter, and you spend a year in jail. Maybe it's as bad as that. You think you can take it on the chin?'

'So you're waiting for me when I come out.'

'I'll be there.'

'Then I can do it.'

'Don't pay any attention to me. I'm a drunk. They got tests that'll show that. I'll say stuff that's cock-eyed. That's to cross them up, so when I'm sober and tell it my way, they'll believe it.'

'I'll remember.'

'And you're pretty sore at me. For being drunk. For being the cause of it all.'

'Yes. I know.'

'Then we're set.'

'Frank.'

'Yes?'

'There's just one thing. We've got to be in love. If we love each other, then nothing matters.'

'Well, do we?'

'I'll be the first one to say it. I love you, Frank.'

'I love you, Cora.'

'Kiss me.'

I kissed her, and held her close, and then I saw a flicker of light on the hill across the ravine.

'Up on the road, now. You're going through with it.'

'I'm going through with it.'

'Just ask for help. You don't know he's dead yet.'

'I know.'

'You fell down, after you climbed out. That's how you got the sand on your clothes.'

'Yes. Goodbye.'

'Goodbye.'

She started up to the road, and I dived for the car. But all of a sudden, I found I didn't have any hat. I had to be in the car, and my hat had to be with me. I began clawing around for it. The car was coming closer and closer. It was only two or three bends away, and I didn't have my hat yet, and I didn't have a mark on me. I gave up, and started for the car. Then I fell down. I had hooked my foot in it. I grabbed it, and jumped in. My weight no sooner went on the floor than it sank and I felt the car turning over on me. That was the last I knew for a while.

*

Next, I was on the ground, and there was a lot of yelling and talking going on around me. My left arm was shooting pain so bad I would yell every time I felt it, and so was my back. Inside my head was a bellow that would get big and go away again. When it did that the ground would fall away, and this stuff I had drunk would come up. I was there and I wasn't there, but I had sense enough to roll around and kick. There was sand on my clothes too, and there had to be a reason.

Next there was a screech in my ears, and I was in an ambulance. A state cop was at my feet, and a doctor was working on my arm. I went out again as soon as I saw it. It was running blood, and between the wrist and the elbow it was bent like a snapped twig. It was broke. When I came out of it again the doctor was still working on it, and I thought about my back. I wiggled my foot and looked at it to see if I was paralyzed. It moved.

The screech kept bringing me out of it, and I looked around, and saw the Greek. He was on the other bunk.

'Yay Nick.'

Nobody said anything. I looked around some more, but I couldn't see anything of Cora.

After a while they stopped, and lifted out the Greek. I waited for them to lift me out, but they didn't. I knew he was really dead, then, and there wouldn't be any cock-eyed stuff this time, selling him a story about a cat. If they had taken us both out, it would be a hospital. But when they just took him out, it was a mortuary.

We went on, then, and when they stopped they lifted me out. They carried me in, and set the stretcher on a wheel table, and rolled me in a white room. Then they got ready to set my arm. They wheeled up a machine to give me gas for that, but then they had an argument. There was another doctor there by that time that said he was the jail physician, and the hospital doctors got pretty sore. I knew what it was about. It was those tests for being drunk. If they gave me the gas first, that would ball up the breath test, the most important one. The jail doctor went out, and made me blow through a glass pipe into some stuff that looked like water but turned yellow when I blew in it. Then he took some blood, and some other samples that he poured in bottles through a funnel. Then they gave me the gas.

When I began to come out of it I was in a room, in bed, and my head was all covered with bandages, and so was my arm, with a sling besides, and my back was all strapped up with adhesive tape so I could hardly move. A state cop was there, reading the morning paper. My head ached like hell, and so did my back, and my arm had shooting pains in it. After a while a nurse came in and gave me a pill, and I went to sleep.

When I woke up it was about noon, and they gave me something to eat. Then two more cops came in, and they put me on a stretcher again, and took me down and put me in another ambulance.

'Where we going?'

'Inquest.'

'Inquest. That's what they have when somebody's dead, ain't it.'

'That's right.'

'I was afraid they'd got it.'

'Only one.'

'Which?'

'The man.'

'Oh. Was the woman bad hurt?'

'Not bad.'

'Looks pretty bad for me, don't it?'

'Watch out there, buddy. It's OK with us if you want to talk, but anything you say may fall back in your lap when you get to court.'

'That's right. Thanks.'

When we stopped it was in front of a undertaker shop in Hollywood, and they carried me in. Cora was there, pretty battered up. She had on a blouse that the police matron had lent her, and it puffed out around her belly like it was stuffed with hay. Her suit and her shoes were dusty, and her eye was all swelled up where I had hit it. She had the police matron with her. The coroner was back of a table, with some kind of a secretary guy beside him. Off to one side were a half dozen guys that acted pretty sore, with cops standing guard over them. They were the jury. There was a bunch of other people, with cops pushing them around to the place where they ought to stand. The undertaker was tip-toeing around, and every now and then he would shove a chair under somebody. He brought a couple for Cora and the matron. Off to one side, on a table, was something under a sheet.

Soon as they had me parked the way they wanted me, on a table, the coroner rapped with his pencil and they started. First thing, was a legal identification. She began to cry when they lifted the sheet off, and I didn't like it much myself. After she looked, and I looked, and the jury looked, they dropped the sheet again.

'Do you know this man?'

'He was my husband.'

'His name?'

'Nick Papadakis.'

Next came the witnesses. The sergeant told how he got the call and went up there with two officers after he phoned for an ambulance, and how he sent Cora in by a car he took charge of, and me and the Greek in by ambulance, and how the Greek died on the way in, and was dropped off at the mortuary. Next, a hick by the name of Wright told how he was coming around the bend, and heard a woman scream, and heard a crash, and saw the car going over and over, the lights still on, down the gully. He saw Cora in the road, waving at him for help, and went down to the car with her and tried to get me and the Greek out. He couldn't do it, because the car was on top of us, so he sent his brother, that was in the car with him, for help. After a while more people came, and the cops, and when the cops took charge they got the car off us and put us in the ambulance. Then Wright's brother told about the same thing, only he went back for the cops.

Then the jail doctor told how I was drunk, and how examination of the stomach showed the Greek was drunk, but Cora wasn't drunk. Then he told which cracked bone it was that the Greek died of. Then the coroner turned to me and asked me if I wanted to testify.

'Yes sir, I guess so.'

'I warn you that any statement you make may be used against you, and that you are under no compulsion to testify unless you so wish.'

'I got nothing to hold back.'

'All right, then. What do you know about this?'

'All I know is that first I was going along. Then I felt the car sink under me, and something hit me, and that's all I can remember until I come to in the hospital.'

'*You* were going along?'

'Yes sir.'

'You mean you were driving the car?'

'Yes sir, I was driving it.'

That was just a cock-eyed story I was going to take back later on, when we got in a place where it really meant something, which this inquest didn't. I figured if I told a bum story first, and then turned around and told another story, it would sound like the second story was really true, where if I had a pat story right from the beginning, it would sound like what it was, pat. I was doing this one different from the first time. I meant to look bad, right from the start. But if I wasn't driving the car, it didn't make any difference how bad I looked, they couldn't do anything to me. What I was afraid of was that perfect murder stuff that we cracked up on last time. Just one little thing, and we were sunk. But here, if I looked bad, there could be quite a few things and still I wouldn't look much worse. The worse I looked on account of being drunk, the less the whole thing would look like a murder.

The cops looked at each other, and the coroner studied me like he thought I was crazy. They had already heard it all, how I was pulled out from under the back seat.

'You're sure of that? That you were driving?'

'Absolutely sure.'

'You had been drinking?'

'No sir.'

'You heard the results of the tests that were given you?'

'I don't know nothing about the tests. All I know is I didn't have no drink.'

He turned to Cora. She said she would tell what she could.

'Who was driving this car?'

'I was.'

'Where was this man?'

'On the back seat.'

'Had he been drinking?'

She kind of looked away, and swallowed, and cried a little bit. 'Do I have to answer that?'

'You don't have to answer any question unless you so wish.'

'I don't want to answer.'

'Very well, then. Tell in your own words what happened.'

'I was driving along. There was a long up-grade, and the car got hot. My husband said I had better stop to let it cool off.'

'How hot?'

'Over 200.'

'Go on.'

'So after we started the down-grade, I cut the motor, and when we got to the bottom it was still hot, and before we started up again we stopped. We were there maybe ten minutes. Then I started up again. And I don't know what happened. I went into high, and didn't get enough power, and I went into second, right quick, and the men were talking, or maybe it was on account of making the quick shift, but anyhow, I felt one side of the car go down. I yelled to them to jump, but it was too late. I felt the car going over and over, and the next thing I knew I was trying to get out, and then I was out, and then I was up on the road.'

The coroner turned to me again. 'What are you trying to do, shield this woman?'

'I don't notice her shielding me any.'

The jury went out, and then came in and gave a verdict that the said Nick Papadakis came to his death as the result of an automobile accident on the Malibu Lake Road, caused in whole or in part by criminal conduct on the part of me and Cora, and recommended that we be held for the action of the grand jury.

There was another cop with me that night, in the hospital, and next morning he told me that Mr Sackett was coming over to see me, and I better get ready. I could hardly move yet, but I had the hospital barber shave me up and make me look as good as he could. I knew who Sackett was. He was the District Attorney. About half past ten he showed up, and the cop went out, and there was nobody there but him and me. He was a big guy with a bald head and a breezy manner.

'Well, well, well. How do you feel?'

'I feel OK, judge. Kind of shook me up a little, but I'll be all right.'

'As the fellow said when he fell out of the airplane, it was a swell ride but we lit kind of hard.'

'That's it.'

'Now, Chambers, you don't have to talk to me if you don't want to, but I've come over here, partly to see what you look like, and partly because it's been my experience that a frank talk saves a lot of breath afterwards, and sometimes paves the way to the disposition of a whole case with a proper plea, and anyway, as the fellow says, after it's over we understand each other.'

'Why sure, judge. What was it you wanted to know?'

I made it sound pretty shifty, and he sat there looking me over. 'Suppose we start at the beginning.'

'About this trip?'

'That's it. I want to hear all about it.'

He got up and began to walk around. The door was right by my bed, and I jerked it open. The cop was halfway down the hall, chinning a nurse. Sackett burst out laughing. 'No, no dictaphones in this. They don't use them anyway, except in movies.'

I let a sheepish grin come over my face. I had him like I wanted him. I had pulled a dumb trick on him, and he had got the better of me. 'OK, judge. I guess it was pretty silly, at that. All right, I'll begin at the beginning and tell it all. I'm in dutch all right, but I guess lying about it won't do any good.'

'That's the right attitude, Chambers.'

I told him how I walked out on the Greek, and how I bumped into him on the street one day, and he wanted me back, and then asked me to go on this Santa Barbara trip with them to talk it over. I told about how we put down the wine, and how we started out, with me at the wheel. He stopped me then.

'So you *were* driving the car?'

'Judge, suppose *you* tell *me* that.'

'What do you mean, Chambers?'

'I mean I heard what she said, at the inquest. I heard what those cops said. I know where they found me. So I know who was driving, all right. She was. But if I tell it like I remember it, I got to say I was driving it. I didn't tell that coroner any lie, judge. *It still seems to me I was driving it.*'

'You lied about being drunk.'

'That's right. I was all full of booze, and ether, and dope that they give you, and I lied all right. But I'm all right now, and I got sense enough to know the truth is all that can get me out of this, if anything can. Sure, I was drunk. I was stinko. And all I could think of was, I mustn't let them know I was drunk, because I was driving the car, and if they find out I was drunk, I'm sunk.'

'Is that what you'd tell a jury?'

'I'd have to, judge. But what I can't understand is how she came to be driving it. I started out with it. I know that. I can even remember a guy standing there laughing at me. Then how come she was driving when it went over?'

'You drove it about two feet.'

'You mean two miles.'

'I mean two feet. Then she took the wheel away from you.'

'Gee, I *must* have been stewed.'

'Well, it's one of those things that a jury might believe. It's just got that cock-eyed look to it that generally goes with the truth. Yes, they might believe it.'

He sat there looking at his nails, and I had a hard time to keep the grin from creeping over my face. I was glad when he started asking me more questions, so I could get my mind on something else, besides how easy I had fooled him.

'When did you go to work for Papadakis, Chambers?'

'Last winter.'

'How long did you stay with him?'

'Till a month ago. Maybe six weeks.'

'You worked for him six months, then?'

'About that.'

'What did you do before that?'

'Oh, knocked around.'

'Hitch-hiked? Rode freights? Bummed your meals wherever you could?'

'Yes sir.'

He unstrapped a briefcase, put a pile of papers on the table, and began looking through them. 'Ever been in Frisco?'

'Born there.'

'Kansas City? New York? New Orleans? Chicago?'

'I've seen them all.'

'Ever been in jail?'

'I have, judge. You knock around, you get in trouble with the cops now and then. Yes sir, I've been in jail.'

'Ever been in jail in Tuscson?'

'Yes sir. I think it was ten days I got there. It was for trespassing on railroad property.'

'Salt Lake City? San Diego? Wichita?'

'Yes sir. All those places.'

'Oakland?'

'I got three months there, judge. I got in a fight with a railroad detective.'

'You beat him up pretty bad, didn't you?'

'Well, as the fellow says, he was beat up pretty bad, but you ought to seen the other one. I was beat up pretty bad, myself.'

'Los Angeles?'

'Once. But that was only three days.'

'Chambers, how did you come to go to work for Papadakis, anyhow?'

'Just a kind of an accident. I was broke, and he needed somebody. I blew in there to get something to eat, and he offered me a job, and I took it.'

'Chambers, does that strike you as funny?'

'I don't know how you mean, judge?'

'That after knocking around all these years, and never doing any work, or even trying to do any, so far as I can see, you suddenly settled down, and went to work, and held a job steady?'

'I didn't like it much, I'll own up to that.'

'But you stuck.'

'Nick, he was one of the nicest guys I ever knew. After I got a stake, I tried to tell him I was through, but I just didn't have the heart, much trouble as he had had with his help. Then when he had the accident, and wasn't there, I blew. I just blew, that's all. I guess I ought to treated him better, but I got rambling feet, judge. When they say go, I got to go with them. I just took a quiet way out.'

'And then, the day after you came back, he got killed.'

'You kind of make me feel bad now, judge. Because maybe I tell the jury different, but I'm telling you now I feel that was a hell of a lot my fault. If I hadn't been there, and begun promoting him for something to drink that afternoon, maybe he'd be here now. Understand, maybe that didn't have anything to do with it at all. I don't know. I was stinko, and I don't know what happened. Just the same, if she hadn't had two drunks in the car, maybe she could have drove better, couldn't she? Anyway, that's how I feel about it.'

I looked at him, to see how he was taking it. He wasn't even looking at me. All of a sudden he jumped up and came over to the bed and took me by the shoulder. 'Out with it, Chambers. Why did you stick with Papadakis for six months?'

'Judge, I don't get you.'

'Yes you do. I've seen her, Chambers, and I can guess why you did it. She was in my office yesterday, and she had a black eye, and was pretty well banged up, but even with that she looked pretty good. For something like that, plenty of guys have said goodbye to the road, rambling feet or not.'

'Anyhow they rambled. No, judge, you're wrong.'

'They didn't ramble long. It's too good, Chambers. Here's

an automobile accident that yesterday was a dead open-and-shut case of manslaughter, and today it's just evaporated into nothing at all. Every place I touch it, up pops a witness to tell me something, and when I fit all they have to say together, I haven't got any case. Come on, Chambers. You and that woman murdered this Greek, and the sooner you own up to it the better it'll be for you.'

There wasn't any grin creeping over my face then, I'm here to tell you. I could feel my lips getting numb, and I tried to speak, but nothing would come out of my mouth.

'Well, why don't you say something?'

'You're coming at me. You're coming at me for something pretty bad. I don't know anything to say, judge.'

'You were gabby enough a few minutes ago, when you were handing me that stuff about the truth being all that would get you out of this. Why can't you talk now?'

'You got me all mixed up.'

'All right, we'll take it one thing at a time, so you won't be mixed up. In the first place, you've been sleeping with that woman, haven't you?'

'Nothing like it.'

'How about the week Papadakis was in the hospital? Where did you sleep then?'

'In my own room.'

'And she slept in hers? Come on, I've seen her, I tell you. I'd have been in there if I had to kick the door down and hang for rape. So would you. So *were* you.'

'I never even thought of it.'

'How about all those trips you took with her to Hasselman's Market in Glendale? What did you do with her on the way back?'

'Nick told me to go on those trips himself.'

'I didn't ask you who told you to go. I asked you what you did.'

I was so groggy I had to do something about it quick. All

I could think of was to get sore. 'All right, suppose we did. We didn't, but you say we did, and we'll let it go at that. Well, if it was all that easy, what would we be knocking him off for? Holy smoke, judge, I hear tell of guys that would commit murder for what you say I was getting, when they weren't getting it, but I never hear tell of a guy that would commit murder for it when he already had it.'

'No? Well I'll tell you what you were knocking him off for. A piece of property out there, for one thing, that Papadakis paid $14,000 for, cash on the nail. And for that other little Christmas present you and she thought you would get on the boat with, and see what the wild waves looked like. *That little $10,000 accident policy that Papadakis carried on his life.*'

I could still see his face, but all around it was getting black and I was trying to keep myself from keeling over in bed. Next thing, he was holding a glass of water to my mouth. 'Have a drink. You'll feel better.'

I drank some of it. I had to.

'Chambers, I think this is the last murder you'll have a hand in for some time, but if you ever try another, for God's sake leave insurance companies out of it. They'll spend five times as much as Los Angeles County will let me put into a case. They've got detectives five times as good as any I'll be able to hire. They know their stuff A to izzard, and they're right on your tail now. It means money to them. That's where you and she made your big mistake.'

'Judge, I hope Christ may kill me, I never heard of an insurance policy until just this minute.'

'You turned white as a sheet.'

'Wouldn't you?'

'Well, how about getting me on your side, right from the start? How about a full confession, a quick plea of guilty, and I'll do what I can for you with the court? Ask for clemency for you both.'

'Nothing doing.'

'How about all that stuff you were telling me just now? About the truth, and how you'd have to come clean with the jury, and all that? You think you can get away with lies now? You think I'm going to stand for that?'

'I don't know what you're going to stand for. To hell with that. You stand for your side of it and I'll stand for mine. I didn't do it, and that's all I stand for. You got that?'

'The hell you say. Getting tough with me, hey? All right, now you get it. You're going to find out what that jury's really going to hear. First, you were sleeping with her, weren't you? Then Papadakis had a little accident, and you and she had a swell time. In bed together at night, down to the beach by day, holding hands and looking at each other in between. Then you both had a swell idea. Now that he's had an accident, make him take out an accident policy, and then knock him off. So you blew, to give her a chance to put it over. She worked at it, and pretty soon she had him. He took out a policy, a real good policy, that covered accidents, and health, and all the rest of it, and cost $46.72. Then you were ready. Two days after that, Frank Chambers accidentally on purpose ran into Nick Papadakis on the street, and Nick tries to get him to go back to work for him. And what do you know about that, he and his wife had it already fixed up they were going to Santa Barbara, had the hotel reservations and everything, so of course there was nothing to it but Frank Chambers had to come with them, just for old times' sake. And you went. You got the Greek a little bit drunk, and did the same for yourself. You stuck a couple of wine bottles in the car, just to get the cops good and sore. Then you had to take that Malibu Lake Road, so she could see Malibu Beach. Wasn't that an idea, now. Eleven o'clock at night, and she was going to drive down there to look at a bunch of houses with waves in front of them. But you didn't get there. You stopped. And while you were stopped, you crowned the

Greek with one of the wine bottles. A beautiful thing to crown a man with, Chambers, and nobody knew it better than you, because that was what you crowned that railroad dick with, over in Oakland. You crowned him, and then she started the car. And while she was climbing out on the running board, you leaned over from behind, and held the wheel, and fed with the hand throttle. It didn't need much gas, because it was in second gear. And after she got on the running board, she took the wheel and fed with the hand throttle, and it was your turn to climb out. But you were just a little drunk, weren't you? You were too slow, and she was a little too quick to shoot the car over the edge. So she jumped and you were caught. You think a jury won't believe that, do you? It'll believe it, because I'll prove every word of it, from the beach trip to the hand throttle, and when I do, there won't be any clemency for you, boy. It'll be the rope, with you hanging on the end of it, and when they cut you down they'll bury you out there with all the others that were too goddam dumb to make a deal when they had the chance to keep their neck from being broke.'

'Nothing like that happened. Not that I know of.'

'What are you trying to tell me? That *she* did it?'

'I'm not trying to tell you that anybody did it. Leave me alone! Nothing like that happened.'

'How do you know? I thought you were stinko.'

'It didn't happen that I know of.'

'Then you mean she did it?'

'I don't mean no such a goddam thing. I mean what I say and that's all I mean.'

'Listen, Chambers. There were three people in the car, you, and she, and the Greek. Well, it's a cinch the Greek didn't do it. If you didn't do it, that leaves her, doesn't it?'

'Who the hell says anybody did it?'

'I do. Now we're getting somewhere, Chambers. Because maybe you didn't do it. You say you're telling the truth, and maybe you are. But if you are telling the truth, and didn't have any interest in this woman except as the wife of a friend, then you've got to do something about it, haven't you? You've got to sign a complaint against her.'

'What do you mean complaint?'

'If she killed the Greek, she tried to kill you too, didn't she? You can't let her get away with that. Somebody might think it was pretty funny if you did. Sure, you'd be a sucker to let her get away with it. She knocks off her husband for the insurance, and she tries to knock off you too. You've got to do something about that, haven't you?'

'I might, if she did it. But I don't know she did it.'

'If I prove it to you, you'll have to sign the complaint, won't you?'

'Sure. *If* you can prove it.'

'All right, I'll prove it. When you stopped, you got out of the car, didn't you?'

'No.'

'What? I thought you were so stinko you didn't remember anything. That's the second time you've remembered something now. I'm surprised at you.'

'Not that I know of.'

'But you did. Listen to this man's statement: "I didn't notice much about the car, except that a woman was at the wheel and one man was inside laughing when we went by, and another man was out back, sick." So you were out back a few minutes, sick. That was when she crowned Papadakis with the bottle. And when you got back you never noticed anything, because you were stinko, and Papadakis had passed out anyhow, and there was hardly anything to notice. You sat back and passed out, and that was when she slid up into second, kept her hand on the hand throttle, fed with that, and as soon as she had slid out on the running board, shot the car over.'

'That don't prove it.'

'Yes it does. The witness Wright says that the car was rolling over and over, down the gully, when he came around the bend, *but the woman was up on the road, waving to him for help!*'

'Maybe she jumped.'

'If she jumped, it's funny she took her handbag with her, isn't it? Chambers, can a woman drive with a handbag in her hand? When she jumps, has she got time to pick it up? Chambers, it can't be done. It's impossible to jump from a sedan car that's turning over into a gully. She wasn't in the car when it went over! That proves it, doesn't it?'

'I don't know.'

'What do you mean you don't know? Are you going to sign that complaint or not?'

'No.'

'Listen, Chambers, it was no accident that car went over a second too soon. It was you or her, and she didn't mean it would be you.'

'Let me alone. I don't know what you're talking about.'

'Boy, it's still you or her. If you didn't have anything to do with this, you better sign this thing. Because if you don't, then I'll know. And so will the jury. And so will the judge. And so will the guy that springs the trap.'

He looked at me a minute, then went out, and came back with another guy. The guy sat down and made out a form with a fountain pen. Sackett brought it over to me. 'Right here, Chambers.'

I signed. There was so much sweat on my hand the guy had to blot it off the paper.

10

After he went, the cop came back and mumbled something about a blackjack. We played a few rounds, but I couldn't get my mind on it. I made out it got on my nerves to deal with one hand, and quit.

'He kind of got to you, hey?'

'Little bit.'

'He's tough, he is. He gets to them all. He looks like a preacher, all full of love for the human race, but he's got a heart like a stone.'

'Stone is right.'

'Only one guy in this town has got it on him.'

'Yeah?'

'Guy named Katz. You've heard of him.'

'Sure, I heard of him.'

'Friend of mine.'

'It's the kind of a friend to have.'

'Say. You ain't supposed to have no lawyer yet. You ain't been arraigned, and you can't send for nobody. They can hold you forty-eight hours incommunicado, they call it. But if he shows up here, I got to let him see you, you get it? He might show up here, if I happened to be talking to him.'

'You mean you get a cut.'

'I mean he's a friend of mine. Well, if he didn't give me no cut, he wouldn't be no friend, would he? He's a great guy.

He's the only one in this town can throw the headlock on Sackett.'

'You're on, kid. And the sooner the better.'

'I'll be back.'

He went out for a little while, and when he came back he gave me a wink. And pretty soon, sure enough, there came a knock on the door, and in came Katz. He was a little guy, about forty years old, with a leathery face and a black moustache, and the first thing he did when he came in was take out a bag of Bull Durham smoking tobacco and a pack of brown papers and roll himself a cigarette. When he lit it, it burned halfway up one side, and that was the last he did about it. It just hung there, out the side of his mouth, and if it was lit or out, or whether he was asleep or awake, I never found out. He just sat there, with his eyes half shut and one leg hung over the arm of the chair, and his hat on the back of his head, and that was all. You might think that was a poor sight to see, for a guy in my spot, but it wasn't. He might be asleep, but even asleep he looked like he knew more than most guys awake, and a kind of a lump came up in my throat. It was like the sweet chariot had swung low and was going to pick me up.

The cop watched him roll the cigarette like it was Cadona doing the triple somersault, and he hated to go, but he had to. After he was out, Katz motioned to me to get going. I told him about how we had an accident, and how Sackett was trying to say we murdered the Greek for the insurance, and how he made me sign that complaint paper that said she had tried to murder me too. He listened, and after I had run down he sat there a while without saying anything. Then he got up.

'He's got you in a spot all right.'

'I ought not to signed it. I don't believe she did any such a goddam thing. But he had me going. And now I don't know where the hell I'm at.'

'Well, anyhow, you ought not to have signed it.'

'Mr Katz, will you do one thing for me? Will you see her, and tell her—'

'I'll see her. And I'll tell her what's good for her to know. For the rest of it, I'm handling this, and that means I'm handling it. You got that?'

'Yes, sir, I've got it.'

'I'll be with you at the arraignment. Or anyhow, somebody that I pick will be with you. As Sackett has made a complainant out of you, I may not be able to appear for you both, but I'll be handling it. And once more, that means that whatever I do, I'm handling it.'

'Whatever you do, Mr Katz.'

'I'll be seeing you.'

That night they put me on a stretcher again, and took me over to court for the arraignment. It was a magistrate's court, not a regular court. There wasn't any jury box, or witness stand, or any of that stuff. The magistrate sat on a platform, with some cops beside him, and in front of him was a long desk that ran clear across the room, and whoever had something to say hooked his chin over the desk and said it. There was a big crowd there, and photographers were snapping flashlights at me when they carried me in, and you could tell from the buzz that something big was going on. I couldn't see much, from down there on the stretcher, but I got a flash at Cora, sitting on the front bench with Katz, and Sackett, off to one side talking to some guys with briefcases, and some of the cops and witnesses that had been at the inquest. They set me down in front of the desk, on a couple of tables they had shoved together, and they hadn't much more than got the blankets spread over me right than they wound up a case about a Chinese woman, and a cop began rapping for quiet. While he was doing that, a young guy leaned down over me, and said his name was White, and Katz had asked him to represent me. I nodded my head, but he kept whispering that Mr Katz had sent him, and the cop got sore and began banging hard.

'Cora Papadakis.'

She stood up, and Katz took her up to the desk. She almost touched me as she went by, and it seemed funny to smell her, the same smell that had always set me wild, in the middle of all this stuff. She looked a little better than she had yesterday. She had on another blouse, that fitted her right, and her suit had been cleaned and pressed, and her shoes had been polished, and her eye was black, but not swelled. All the other people went up with her, and after they had spread out in line, the cop told them to raise their right hand, and began to mumble about the truth, the whole truth, and nothing but the truth. He stopped in the middle of it to look down and see if I had my right hand raised. I didn't. I shoved it up, and he mumbled all over again. We all mumbled back.

The magistrate took off his glasses, and told Cora she was charged with the murder of Nick Papadakis, and with assault against Frank Chambers, with intent to kill, that she could make a statement if she wanted to, but any statement she made could be used against her, that she had the right to be represented by counsel, that she had eight days to plead, and the court would hear her plea at any time during that period. It was a long spiel, and you could hear them coughing before he got done.

Then Sackett started up, and told what he was going to prove. It was about the same as he had told me that morning, only he made it sound solemn as hell. When he got through, he began putting on his witnesses. First there was the ambulance doctor, that told when the Greek had died, and where. Then came the jail doctor, that had made the autopsy, and then came the coroner's secretary, that identified the minutes of the inquest, and left them with the magistrate, and then came a couple of more guys, but I forget what they said.

When they got done, all that the whole bunch had proved was that the Greek was dead, and as I knew that anyway, I didn't pay much attention. Katz never asked any of them anything. Every time the magistrate would look at him, he would wave his hand and the guy would step aside.

After they had the Greek dead enough to suit them, Sackett really straightened out, and put some stuff in that meant something. He called a guy that said he represented the Pacific States Accident Assurance Corporation of America, and he told how the Greek had taken out a policy just five days before. He told what it covered, how the Greek would get $25 a week for 52 weeks if he got sick, and the same if he got hurt in an accident so he couldn't work, and how he would get $5,000 if he lost one limb, and $10,000 if he lost two limbs, and how his widow would get $10,000 if he was killed in an accident, and $20,000 if the accident was on a railroad train. When he got that far it began to sound like a sales talk, and the magistrate held up his hand.

'I've got all the insurance I need.'

Everybody laughed at the magistrate's gag. Even I laughed. You'd be surprised how funny it sounded.

Sackett asked a few more questions, and then the magistrate turned to Katz. Katz thought a minute, and when he talked to the guy, he did it slow, like he wanted to make sure he had every word straight.

'You are an interested party to this proceeding?'

'In a sense I am, Mr Katz.'

'You wish to escape payment of this indemnity, on the ground that a crime has been committed, is that correct?'

'That is correct.'

'You really believe that a crime has been committed, that this woman killed her husband to obtain this indemnity, and either tried to kill this man, or else deliberately placed him in jeopardy that might cause his death, all as part of a plan to obtain this indemnity?'

The guy kind of smiled, and thought a minute, like he would return the compliment and get every word straight too. 'Answering that question, Mr Katz, I would say I've handled thousands of such cases, cases of fraud that go over my desk every day, and I think I have an unusual experience in that kind of investigation. I may say that I have never seen a clearer case in all my years' work for this and other companies. I don't only believe a crime has been committed, Mr Katz. I practically know it.'

'That is all. Your honor, I plead her guilty on both charges.'

If he had dropped a bomb in that courtroom, he couldn't have stirred it up quicker. Reporters rushed out, and photographers rushed up to the desk to get pictures. They kept bumping into each other, and the magistrate got sore and began banging for order. Sackett looked like he had been shot, and all over the place there was a roar like somebody had all of a sudden shoved a seashell up against your ear. I kept trying to see Cora's face. But all I could get of it was the corner of her mouth. It kept twitching, like somebody was jabbing a needle into it about once every second.

Next thing I knew, the guys on the stretcher picked me up, and followed the young guy, White, out of the courtroom. Then they went with me on the double across a couple of halls into a room with three or four cops in it. White said something about Katz, and the cops cleared out. They set me down on the desk, and then the guys on the stretcher went out. White walked around a little, and then the door opened and a matron came in with Cora. Then White and the matron went out, and the door closed, and we were alone. I tried to think of something to say, and couldn't. She walked around, and didn't look at me. Her mouth was still twitching. I kept swallowing, and after a while I thought of something.

'We've been flim-flammed, Cora.'

She didn't say anything. She just kept walking around.

'That guy Katz, he's nothing but a cop's stool. A cop sent him to me. I thought he was on the up-and-up. But we've been flim-flammed.'

'Oh no, we ain't been flim-flammed.'

'We been flim-flammed. I ought to have known, when the cop tried to sell him to me. But I didn't. I thought he was on the level.'

'I've been flim-flammed, but you haven't.'

'Yes I have. He fooled me too.'

'I see it all now. I see why I had to drive the car. I see it, that other time, why it was me that had to do it, not you. Oh yes, I fell for you because you were smart. And now I find out you're smart. Ain't that funny? You fall for a guy because he's smart and then you find out he's smart.'

'What are you trying to tell me, Cora?'

'Flim-flammed! I'll say I was. You and that lawyer. You fixed it up all right. You fixed it up so I tried to kill you too. That was so it would look like you couldn't have had anything to do with it. Then you have me plead guilty in court. So you're not in it at all. All right. I guess I'm pretty dumb. But I'm not that dumb. Listen, Mr Frank Chambers. When I get through, just see how smart you are. There's just such a thing as being too smart.'

I tried to talk to her, but it wasn't any use. When she had got so that even her lips were white, under the lipstick, the door opened and Katz came in. I tried to jump for him, off the stretcher. I couldn't move. They had me strapped so I couldn't move.

'Get out of here, you goddam stool. *You* were handling it. I'll say you were. But now I know you for what you are. Do you hear that? Get out of here!'

'Why, what's the matter, Chambers?'

You would have thought he was a Sunday school teacher, talking to some kid that was crying for his chewing gum that had been taken away. 'Why, what's the matter? I *am* handling it. I told you that.'

'That's right. Only God help you if I ever get you so I got my hands on you.'

He looked at her, like it was something he just couldn't understand, and maybe she could help him out. She came over to him.

'This man here, this man and you, you ganged up on me so I would get it and he would go free. Well, he was in this as much as I was, and he's not going to get away with it. I'm going to tell it. I'm going to tell it all, and I'm going to tell it right now.'

He looked at her, and shook his head, and it was the phoniest look I ever saw on a man's face. 'Now my dear. I wouldn't do that. If you'll just let me handle this—'

'You handled it. Now I'll handle it.'

He got up, shrugged his shoulders, and went out. He was hardly gone before a guy with big feet and a red neck came in with a little portable typewriter, set it on a chair with a couple of books under it, hitched up to it, and looked at her.

'Mr Katz said you wanted to make a statement?'

He had a little squeaky voice, and a kind of a grin when he talked.

'That's right. A statement.'

She began to speak jerky, two or three words at a time, and as fast as she said it, he rattled it off on the typewriter. She told it all. She went back to the beginning, and told how she met me, how we first began going together, how we tried to knock off the Greek once, but missed. A couple of times, a cop put his head in at the door, but the guy at the typewriter held up his hand.

'Just a few minutes, sarge.'

'OK.'

When she got to the end, she said she didn't know

anything about the insurance, we hadn't done it for that at all, but just to get rid of him.

'That's all.'

He gathered his sheets together, and she signed them. 'Will you just initial these pages?' She initialed them. He got out a notary stamp, and made her hold up her right hand, and put the stamp on, and signed it. Then he put the papers in his pocket, closed his typewriter, and went out.

She went to the door and called the matron. 'I'm ready now.' The matron came in and took her out. The guys on the stretcher came in and carried me out. They went on the double, but on the way they got jammed in with the crowd that was watching her, where she was standing in front of the elevators with the matron, waiting to go up to the jail. It's on the top floor of the Hall of Justice. They pushed on through, and my blanket got pulled so it was trailing on the floor. She picked it up and tucked it around me, then turned away quick.

11

They took me back to the hospital, but instead of the state cop watching me, it was this guy that had taken the confession. He lay down on the other bed. I tried to sleep, and after a while I did. I dreamed she was looking at me, and I was trying to say something to her, but couldn't. Then she would go down, and I would wake up, and that crack would be in my ears, that awful crack that the Greek's head made when I hit it. Then I would sleep again, and dream I was falling. And I would wake up again, holding on to my neck, and that same crack would be in my ears. One time when I woke up I was yelling. He leaned up on his elbow.

'Yay.'

'Yay.'

'What's the matter?'

'Nothing's the matter. Just had a dream.'

'OK.'

He never left me for a minute. In the morning, he made them bring him a basin of water, and took out a razor from his pocket, and shaved. Then he washed himself. They brought in breakfast, and he ate his at the table. We didn't say anything.

They brought me a paper, then, and there it was, with a big picture of Cora on the front page, and a smaller picture of me on the stretcher underneath it. It called her the bottle killer. It told how she had pleaded guilty at the arraignment, and would come up for sentence today. On one of the inside pages, it had a story that it was believed the case would set a record for speed in its disposition, and another story about a preacher that said if all cases were railroaded through that quick, it would do more to prevent crime than passing a hundred laws. I looked all through the paper for something about the confession. It wasn't in there.

About twelve o'clock a young doctor came in and went to work on my back with alcohol, sopping off some of the adhesive tape. He was supposed to sop it off, but most of the time he just peeled it, and it hurt like hell. After he got part of it off, I found I could move. He left the rest on, and a nurse brought me my clothes. I put them on. The guys on the stretcher came in and helped me to the elevator and out of the hospital. There was a car waiting there, with a chauffeur. The guy that had spent the night with me put me in, and we drove about two blocks. Then he took me out, and we went in an office building, and up to an office. And there was Katz with his hand stuck out and a grin all over his face.

'It's all over.'

'Swell. When do they hang her?'

'They don't hang her. She's out, free. Free as a bird. She'll be over in a little while, soon as they fix up some things in court. Come in. I'll tell you about it.'

He took me in a private office and closed the door. Soon as he rolled a cigarette, and half burned it up, and got it pasted on his mouth, he started to talk. I hardly knew him. It didn't seem that a man that had looked so sleepy the day before could be as excited as he was.

'Chambers, this is the greatest case I ever had in my life. I'm in it, and out of it, in less than twenty-four hours, and yet I tell you I never had anything like it. Well, the Dempsey-Firpo fight lasted less than two rounds, didn't it? It's not how long it lasts. It's what you do while you're in there.

'This wasn't really a fight, though. It was a four-handed card game, where every player has been dealt a perfect hand. Beat that, if you can. You think it takes a card player to play a bum hand, don't you. To hell with that. I get those bum hands every day. Give me one like this, where they've all got cards, *where they've all got cards that'll win if they play them right*, and then watch me. Oh, Chambers, you did me a favor all right when you called me in on this. I'll never get another one like it.'

'You haven't said anything yet.'

'I'll say it, don't worry about that. But you won't get it, and you won't know how the hand was played, until I get the cards straightened out for you. Now first. There were you and the woman. You each held a perfect hand. Because that was a perfect murder, Chambers. Maybe you don't even know how good it was. All that stuff Sackett tried to scare you with, about her not being in the car when it went over, and having her handbag with her, and all that, that didn't amount to a goddam thing. A car can teeter before it goes over, can't it? And a woman can grab her handbag before she jumps, can't she? That don't prove any crime. That just proves she's a woman.'

'How'd you find out about that stuff?'

'I got it from Sackett. I had dinner with him last night, and he was crowing over me. He was pitying me, the sap. Sackett and I are enemies. We're the friendliest enemies that ever were. He'd sell his soul to the devil to put something over on me, and I'd do the same for him. We even put up a bet on it. We bet $100. He was giving me the razz, because he had a perfect case, where he could just play the cards and let the hangman do his stuff.'

That was swell, two guys betting $100 on what the

hangman would do to me and Cora, but I wanted to get it straight, just the same.

'If we had a perfect hand, where did his hand come in?'

'I'm getting to that. You had a perfect hand, but Sackett knows that no man and no woman that ever lived could play that hand, not if the prosecutor plays his hand right. He knows that all he's got to do is get one of you working against the other, and it's in the bag. That's the first thing. Next thing, he doesn't even have to work the case up. He's got an insurance company to do that for him, so he doesn't have to lift a finger. That's what Sackett loved about it. All he had to do was play the cards, and the pot would fall right in his lap. So what does he do? He takes this stuff the insurance company dug up for him, and scares the hell out of you with it, and gets you to sign a complaint against her. He takes the best card you've got, which is how bad you were hurt yourself, and makes you trump your own ace with it. If you were hurt that bad, it had to be an accident, and yet Sackett uses that to make you sign a complaint against her. And you sign it, because you're afraid if you don't sign it he'll know goddam well you did it.'

'I turned yellow, that's all.'

'Yellow is a color you figure on in murder, and nobody figures on it better than Sackett. All right. He's got you where he wants you. He's going to make you testify against her, and he knows that once you do that, no power on earth can keep her from ratting on you. So that's where he's sitting when he has dinner with me. He razzes me. He pities me. He bets me $100. And all the time I'm sitting there with a hand that I know I can beat him with, if I only play the cards right. All right, Chambers. You're looking in my hand. What do you see in it?'

'Not much.'

'Well, what?'

'Nothing, to tell you the truth.'

'Neither did Sackett. But now watch. After I left you yesterday, I went to see her, and got an authorization from her to open Papadakis's safe deposit box. And I found what I expected. There were some other policies in that box, and I went to see the agent that wrote them, and this is what I found out:

'That accident policy didn't have anything to do with that accident that Papadakis had a few weeks ago. The agent had turned up on his calendar that Papadakis's automobile insurance had pretty near run out, and he went out there to see him. She wasn't there. They fixed it up pretty quick for the automobile insurance, fire, theft, collision, public liability, the regular line. Then the agent showed Papadakis where he was covered on everything but injury to himself, and asked him how about a personal accident policy. Papadakis got interested right away. Maybe that other accident was the reason for that, but if it was the agent didn't know anything about it. He signed up for the whole works, and gave the agent his check, and next day the policies were mailed out to him. You understand, an agent works for a lot of companies, and not all these policies were written by the same company. That's No. 1 point that Sackett forgot. But the main thing to remember is that Papadakis didn't only have the new insurance. He had the old policies too, *and they still had a week to run.*

'All right, now, get this set-up. The Pacific States Accident is on a $10,000 personal accident policy. The Guaranty of California is on a $10,000 new public liability bond, and the Rocky Mountain Fidelity is on an old $10,000 public liability bond. So that's my first card. He had an insurance company working for him up to $10,000. I had two insurance companies working for me up to $20,000, whenever I wanted to call them in. Do you get it?'

'No, I don't.'

'Look. Sackett stole your big card off you, didn't he? Well,

I stole the same card off him. You were hurt, weren't you? You were hurt bad. Well, if Sackett convicts her of murder, and you bring suit against her for injuries sustained as a result of that murder, then a jury will give you whatever you ask for. And those two bonding companies are liable for every cent of their policies to satisfy that judgment.'

'Now I get it.'

'Pretty, Chambers, pretty. I found that card in my mitt, but you didn't find it, and Sackett didn't find it, and the Pacific States Accident didn't find it, because they were so busy playing Sackett's game for him, and so sure his game would win, that they didn't even think of it.'

He walked around the room a few times, falling for himself every time he passed a little mirror that was in the corner, and then he went on.

'All right, there it was, but the next thing was how to play it. I had to play it quick, because Sackett had already played his, and that confession was due any minute. It might even come at the arraignment, as soon as she heard you testify against her. I had to move fast. So what did I do? I waited till the Pacific States Accident man had testified, and then got him on record that he really believed a crime had been committed. That was just in case I had a false arrest action against him later on. And then, wham, I pleaded her guilty. That ended the arraignment, and for that night, blocked off Sackett. Then I rushed her in a counsel room, claimed a half hour before she was locked up for the night, and sent you in there with her. Five minutes with you was all she needed. When I got in there she was ready to spill it. Then I sent Kennedy in.'

'The dick that was with me last night?'

'He used to be a dick, but he's not a dick any more. He's my gum-shoe man now. She thought she was talking to a dick, but she was really talking to a dummy. But it did the work. After she got it off her chest, she kept quiet till today, and that was long enough. The next thing was you. What you would do was blow. There was no charge against you, so you weren't under arrest any more, even if you thought you were. Soon as you tumbled to that, I knew no tape, or sore back, or hospital orderly, or anything else would hold you, so after he got done with her I sent Kennedy over to keep an eye on you. The next thing was the little midnight conference between the Pacific States Accident, the Guaranty of California, and the Rocky Mountain Fidelity. And when I laid it in front of them, they did business awful quick.'

'What do you mean, they did business?'

'First, I read them the law. I read them the guest clause, Section 141¾, California Vehicle Act. That says if a guest in an automobile gets hurt, he has no right of recovery, *provided*, that if his injury resulted from intoxication or willful misconduct on the part of the driver, then he can recover. You see, you were a guest, and I had pleaded her guilty to murder and assault. Plenty of willful misconduct there, wasn't there? And they couldn't be sure, you know. Maybe she did do it alone. So those two companies on the liability policies, the ones that had their chin hanging out for a wallop from you, they chipped in $5,000 apiece to pay the Pacific States Accident policy, and the Pacific States Accident agreed to pay up and shut up, and the whole thing didn't take over a half hour.'

He stopped and grinned at himself some more.

'What then?'

'I'm still thinking about it. I can still see Sackett's face just now when the Pacific States Accident fellow went on the stand today and said his investigation had convinced him that no crime had been committed, and his company was paying the accident claim in full. Chambers, do you know what that feels like? To feint a guy open and then let him have it, right on the chin? There's no feeling like it in the world.'

'I still don't get it. What was this guy testifying again for?'

'She was up for sentence. And after a plea of guilty, a court

79

usually wants to hear some testimony to find out what the case is really about. To determine the sentence. And Sackett had started in howling for blood. He wanted the death penalty. Oh, he's a blood-thirsty lad, Sackett is. That's why it stimulates me to work against him. He really believes hanging them does some good. You're playing for stakes when you're playing against Sackett. So he put his insurance man on the stand again. But instead of it being *his* son of a bitch, after that little midnight session it was *my* son of a bitch, only Sackett didn't know it. He roared plenty when he found it out. But it was too late. If an insurance company didn't believe she was guilty, a jury would never believe it, would it? There wasn't a chance in the world of convicting her after that. And that was when I burned Sackett. I got up and made a speech to the court. I took my time about it. I told how my client had protested her innocence from the beginning. I told how I didn't believe it. I told how I knew there existed what I regarded as overwhelming evidence against her, enough to convict her in any court, and that I believed I was acting in her best interest when I decided to plead her guilty and throw her on the mercy of the court. But, Chambers, do you know how I rolled that *but* under my tongue? But, in the light of the testimony just given, there was no course open to me but to withdraw the pleas of guilty and allow the cases to proceed. Sackett couldn't do a thing, because I was still within the limit of eight days for a plea. He knew he was sunk. He consented to a plea for manslaughter, the court examined the other witnesses itself, gave her six months, suspended sentence, and practically apologized even for that. We quashed the assault charge. That was the key to the whole thing, and we almost forgot it.'

There came a rap on the door. Kennedy brought Cora in, put some papers down in front of Katz, and left. 'There you are, Chambers. Just sign that, will you? It's a waiver of damages for any injuries sustained by you. It's what they get out of it for being so nice.'

I signed.

'You want me to take you home, Cora?'

'I guess so.'

'One minute, one minute, you two. Not so fast. There's one other little thing. That ten thousand dollars you get for knocking off the Greek.'

She looked at me and I looked at her. He sat there looking at the check. 'You see, it wouldn't be a perfect hand if there hadn't been some money in it for Katz. I forgot to tell you about that. Well. Oh, well. I won't be a hog. I generally take it all, but on this, I'll just make it half. Mrs Papadakis, you make out your check for $5,000, and I'll make this over to you and go over to the bank and fix up the deposits. Here. Here's a blank check.'

She sat down, and picked up the pen, and started to write, and then stopped, like she couldn't quite figure out what it was all about. All of a sudden, he went over and picked up the blank check and tore it up.

'What the hell. Once in a lifetime, isn't it? Here. You keep it all. I don't care about the ten grand. I've got ten grand. This is what I want!'

He opened his pocketbook, took out a slip, and showed it to us. It was Sackett's check for $100. 'You think I'm going to cash that? I am like hell. I'm going to frame it. It goes up there, right over my desk.'

12

We went out of there, and got a cab, because I was so crippled up, and first we went to the bank, and put the check in, and then we went to a flower shop, and got two big bunches of flowers, and then we went to the funeral of the Greek. It seemed funny he was only dead two days, and they were just burying him. The funeral was at a little Greek church, and a big crowd of people was there, some of them Greeks I had seen out to the place now and then. They gave her a dead pan when we came in, and put her in a seat about three rows from the front. I could see them looking at us, and I wondered what I would do if they tried to pull some rough stuff later. They were his friends, not ours. But pretty soon I saw an afternoon paper being passed around, that had big headlines in it that she was innocent, and an usher took a look at it, and came running over and moved us up on the front bench. The guy that did the preaching started out with some dirty cracks about how the Greek died, but a guy went up and whispered to him, and pointed at the paper that had got up near the front by that time, and he turned around and said it all over again, without any dirty cracks, and put in about the sorrowing widow and friends, and they all nodded their heads it was OK. When we went out in the churchyard, where the grave was, a couple of them took her by the arm, and helped her out, and a couple more helped me. I got to blubbering while they were letting him down. Singing those hymns will do it to you every time, and specially when it's about a guy you like as well as I liked the Greek. At the end they sang some song I had heard him sing a hundred times, and that finished me. It was all I could do to lay our flowers out the way they were supposed to go.

The taxi driver found a guy that would rent us a Ford for $15 a week, and we took it, and started out. She drove. When we got out of the city we passed a house that was being built, and all the way out we talked about how not many of them have gone up lately, but the whole section is going to be built up as soon as things get better. When we got out to the place she let me out, put the car away, and then we went inside. It was all just like we left it, even to the glasses in the sink that we had drunk the wine out of, and the Greek's guitar, that hadn't been put away yet because he was so drunk. She put the guitar in the case, and washed the glasses, and then went upstairs. After a minute I went up after her.

She was in their bedroom, sitting by the window, looking out at the road.

'Well?'

She didn't say anything. I started to leave.

'I didn't ask you to leave.'

I sat down again. It was a long while before she snapped out of it.

'You turned on me, Frank.'

'No I didn't. He had me, Cora. I had to sign his paper. If I didn't, then he would tumble to everything. I didn't turn on you. I just went along with him, till I could find out where I was at.'

'You turned on me. I could see it in your eye.'

'All right, Cora, I did. I just turned yellow, that's all. I didn't want to do it. I tried not to do it. But he beat me down. I cracked up, that's all.'

'I know.'

'I went through hell about it.'

'And I turned on you, Frank.'

'They made you do it. You didn't want to. They set a trap for you.'

'I wanted to do it. I hated you then.'

'That's all right. It was for something I didn't really do. You know how it was, now.'

'No. I hated you for something you really did.'

'I never hated you, Cora. I hated myself.'

'I don't hate you now. I hate that Sackett. And Katz. Why couldn't they leave us alone? Why couldn't they let us fight it out together? I wouldn't have minded that. I wouldn't have minded it even if it meant – you know. We would have had our love. And that's all we ever had. But the very first time they started their meanness, you turned on me.'

'And you turned on me, don't forget that.'

'That's the awful part. I turned on you. We both turned on each other.'

'Well, that makes it even, don't it?'

'It makes it even, but look at us now. We were up on a mountain. We were up so high, Frank. We had it all, out there, that night. I didn't know I could feel anything like that. And we kissed and sealed it so it would be there forever, no matter what happened. We had more than any two people in the world. And then we fell down. First you, and then me. Yes, it makes it even. We're down here together. But we're not up high any more. Our beautiful mountain is gone.'

'Well what the hell? We're together, ain't we?'

'I guess so. But I thought an awful lot, Frank. Last night. About you and me, and the movies, and why I flopped, and the hash house, and the road, and why you like it. We're just two punks, Frank. God kissed us on the brow that night. He

84

gave us all that two people can ever have. And we just weren't the kind that could have it. We had all that love, and we just cracked up under it. It's a big airplane engine, that takes you through the sky, right up to the top of the mountain. But when you put it in a Ford, it just shakes it to pieces. That's what we are, Frank, a couple of Fords. God is up there laughing at us.'

'The hell he is. Well we're laughing at him too, aren't we? He put up a red stop sign for us, and we went past it. And then what? Did we get shoved off the deep end? We did like hell. We got away clean, and got $10,000 for doing the job. So God kissed us on the brow, did he? Then the devil went to bed with us, and believe you me, kid, he sleeps pretty good.'

'Don't talk that way, Frank.'

'Did we get that ten grand, or didn't we?'

'I don't want to think about the ten grand. It's a lot, but it couldn't buy our mountain.'

'Mountain, hell, we got the mountain and ten thousand smackers to pile on top of that yet. If you want to go up high, take a look around from that pile.'

'You nut. I wish you could see yourself, yelling with that bandage on your head.'

'You forgot something. We got something to celebrate. We ain't never had that drunk yet.'

'I wasn't talking about that kind of a drunk.'

'A drunk's a drunk. Where's that liquor I had before I left?'

I went to my room and got the liquor. It was a quart of Bourbon, three quarters full. I went down, got some Coca Cola glasses, and ice cubes, and White Rock, and came back upstairs. She had taken her hat off and let her hair down. I fixed two drinks. They had some White Rock in them, and a couple of pieces of ice, but the rest was out of the bottle.

'Have a drink. You'll feel better. That's what Sackett said when he put the spot on me, the louse.'

'My, but that's strong.'

'You bet it is. Here, you got too many clothes on.'

I pushed her over to the bed. She held on to her glass, and some of it spilled. 'The hell with it. Plenty more where that came from.'

I began slipping off her blouse. 'Rip me, Frank. Rip me like you did that night.'

I ripped all her clothes off. She twisted and turned, slow, so they would slip out from under her. Then she closed her eyes and lay back on the pillow. Her hair was falling over her shoulders in snaky curls. Her eye was all black, and her breasts weren't drawn up and pointing up at me, but soft, and spread out in two big pink splotches. She looked like the great grandmother of every whore in the world. The devil got his money's worth that night.

13

We kept that up for six months. We kept it up, and it was always the same way. We'd have a fight, and I'd reach for the bottle. What we had the fights about was going away. We couldn't leave the state until the suspended sentence was up, but after that I meant we should blow. I didn't tell her, but I wanted her a long way from Sackett. I was afraid if she got sore at me for something, she'd go off her nut and spill it like she had that other time, after the arraignment. I didn't trust her for a minute. At first, she was all hot for going too, specially when I got talking about Hawaii and the South Seas, but then the money began to roll in. When we opened up, about a week after the funeral, people flocked out there to see what she looked like, and then they came back because they had a good time. And she got all excited about here was our chance to make some more money.

'Frank, all these roadside joints around here are lousy. They're run by people that used to have a farm back in Kansas or somewhere, and got as much idea how to entertain people as a pig has. I believe if somebody came along that knew the business like I do, and tried to make it nice for them, they'd come and bring all their friends.'

'To hell with them. We're selling out anyhow.'

'We could sell easier if we were making money.'

'We're making money.'

'I mean good money. Listen, Frank. I've got an idea people would be glad of the chance to sit out under the trees. Think of that. All this nice weather in California, and what do they do with it? Bring people inside of a joint that's set up ready-made by the Acme Lunch Room Fixture Company, and stinks so it makes you sick to your stomach, and feed them awful stuff that's the same from Fresno down to the border, and never give them any chance to feel good at all.'

'Look. We're selling out, aren't we? Then the less we got to sell the quicker we get rid of it. Sure, they'd like to sit under the trees. Anybody but a California Bar-B-Q slinger would know that. But if we put them under the trees we've got to get tables, and wire up a lot of lights out there, and all that stuff, and maybe the next guy don't want it that way at all.'

'We've got to stay six months. Whether we like it or not.'

'Then we use that six months finding a buyer.'

'I want to try it.'

'All right, then try it. But I'm telling you.'

'I could use some of our inside tables.'

'I said try it, didn't I? Come on. We'll have a drink.'

What we had the big blow-off over was the beer license, and then I tumbled to what she was really up to. She put the tables out under the trees, on a little platform she had built, with a striped awning over them and lanterns at night, and it went pretty good. She was right about it. Those people really enjoyed a chance to sit out under the trees for a half hour, and listen to a little radio music, before they got in their cars and went on. And then beer came back. She saw a chance to leave it just like it was, put beer in, and call it a beer garden.

'I don't want any beer garden, I tell you. All I want is a guy that'll buy the whole works and pay cash.'

'But it seems a shame.'

'Not to me it don't.'

'But look, Frank. The license is only twelve dollars for six months. My goodness, we can afford twelve dollars, can't we?'

'We get the license and then we're in the beer business. We're in the gasoline business already, and the hot dog business, and now we got to go in the beer business. The hell with it. I want to get out of it, not get in deeper.'

'Everybody's got one.'

'And welcome, so far as I'm concerned.'

'People wanting to come, and the place all fixed up under the trees, and now I have to tell them we don't have beer because we haven't any license.'

'Why do you have to tell them anything?'

'All we've got to do is put in coils and then we can have draught beer. It's better than bottled beer, and there's more money in it. I saw some lovely glasses in Los Angeles the other day. Nice tall ones. The kind people like to drink beer out of.'

'So we got to get coils and glasses now, have we? I tell you I don't *want* any beer garden.'

'Frank, don't you ever want to *be* something?'

'Listen, get this. I want to get away from this place. I want to go somewhere else, where every time I look around I don't see the ghost of a goddam Greek jumping out at me, and hear his echo in my dreams, and jump every time the radio comes out with a guitar. I've got to go away, do you hear me? I've got to get out of here, or I go nuts.'

'You're lying to me.'

'Oh no, I'm not lying. I never meant anything more in my life.'

'You don't see the ghost of any Greek, that's not it. Somebody else might see it, but not Mr Frank Chambers. No, you want to go away just because you're a bum, that's all. That's what you were when you came here, and that's what you are now. When we go away, and our money's all gone, then what?'

'What do I care? We go away, don't we?'

'That's it, you don't care. We could stay here—'

'I knew it. That's what you really mean. That's what you've meant all along. That we stay here.'

'And why not? We've got it good. Why wouldn't we stay here? Listen, Frank. You've been trying to make a bum out of me ever since you've known me, but you're not going to do it. I told you, I'm not a bum. I want to *be* something. We stay here. We're not going away. We take out the beer license. We amount to something.'

It was late at night, and we were upstairs, half undressed. She was walking around like she had that time after the arraignment, and talking in the same funny jerks.

'Sure we stay. We do whatever you say, Cora. Here, have a drink.'

'I don't want a drink.'

'Sure you want a drink. We got to laugh some more about getting the money, haven't we?'

'We already laughed about it.'

'But we're going to make more money, aren't we? On the beer garden? We got to put down a couple on that, just for luck.'

'You nut. All right. Just for luck.'

That's the way it went, two or three times a week. And the tip-off was that every time I would come out of a hangover, I would be having those dreams. I would be falling, and that crack would be in my ears.

Right after the sentence ran out, she got the telegram her mother was sick. She got some clothes in a hurry, and I put her on the train, and going back to the parking lot I felt funny, like I was made of gas and would float off somewhere.

I felt free. For a week, anyway, I wouldn't have to wrangle, or fight off dreams, or nurse a woman back to a good humor with a bottle of liquor.

On the parking lot a girl was trying to start her car. It wouldn't do anything. She stepped on everything and it was just plain dead.

'What's the matter? Won't it go?'

'They left the ignition on when they parked it, and now the battery's run out.'

'Then it's up to them. They've got to charge it for you.'

'Yes, but I've got to get home.'

'I'll take you home.'

'You're awfully friendly.'

'I'm the friendliest guy in the world.'

'You don't even know where I live.'

'I don't care.'

'It's pretty far. It's in the country.'

'The further the better. Wherever it is, it's right on my way.'

'You make it hard for a nice girl to say no.'

'Well then, if it's so hard, don't say it.'

She was a light-haired girl, maybe a little older than I was, and not bad on looks. But what got me was how friendly she was, and how she wasn't any more afraid of what I might do to her than if I was a kid or something. She knew her way around all right, you could see that. And what finished it was when I found out she didn't know who I was. We told our names on the way out, and to her mine didn't mean a thing. Boy oh boy what a relief that was. One person in the world that wasn't asking me to sit down to the table a minute, and then telling me to give them the lowdown on that case where they said the Greek was murdered. I looked at her, and I felt the same way I had walking away from the train, like I was made of gas, and would float out from behind the wheel.

'So your name is Madge Allen, hey?'

'Well, it's really Kramer, but I took my own name again after my husband died.'

'Well listen Madge Allen, or Kramer, or whatever you want to call it, I've got a little proposition to make you.'

'Yes?'

'What do you say we turn this thing around, point her south, and you and me take a little trip for about a week?'

'Oh, I couldn't do that?'

'Why not?'

'Oh, I just couldn't, that's all.'

'You like me?'

'Sure I like you.'

'Well, I like you. What's stopping us?'

She started to say something, didn't say it, and then laughed. 'I own up. I'd like to, all right. And if it's something I'm supposed not to do, why that don't mean a thing to me. But I can't. It's on account of the cats.'

'Cats?'

'We've got a lot of cats. And I'm the one that takes care of them. That's why I had to get home.'

'Well, they got pet farms, haven't they? We'll call one up, and tell them to come over and get them.'

That struck her funny. 'I'd like to see a pet farm's face when it saw them. They're not that kind.'

'Cats are cats, ain't they?'

'Not exactly. Some are big and some are little. Mine are big. I don't think a pet farm would do very well with that lion we've got. Or the tigers. Or the puma. Or the three jaguars. They're the worst. A jaguar is an awful cat.'

'Holy smoke. What do you do with those things?'

'Oh, work them in movies. Sell the cubs. People have private zoos. Keep them around. They draw trade.'

'They wouldn't draw my trade.'

'We've got a restaurant. People look at them.'

'Restaurant, hey. That's what I've got. Whole goddam country lives selling hot dogs to each other.'

'Well, anyway, I couldn't walk out on my cats. They've got to eat.'

'The hell we can't. We'll call up Goebel and tell him to come get them. He'll board the whole bunch while we're gone for a hundred bucks.'

'Is it worth a hundred bucks to you to take a trip with me?'

'It's worth exactly a hundred bucks.'

'Oh my. I can't say no to that. I guess you better call up Goebel.'

I dropped her off at her place, found a pay station, called up Goebel, went back home, and closed up. Then I went back after her. It was about dark. Goebel had sent a truck over, and I met it coming back, full of stripes and spots. I parked about a hundred yards down the road, and in a minute she showed up with a little grip, and I helped her in, and we started off.

'You like it?'

'I love it.'

We went down to Caliente, and next day we kept on down the line to Ensenada, a little Mexican town about seventy miles down the coast. We went to a little hotel there, and spent three or four days. It was pretty nice. Ensenada is all Mex, and you feel like you left the USA a million miles away. Our room had a little balcony in front of it, and in the afternoon we would just lay out there, look at the sea, and let the time go by.

'Cats, hey. What do you do, train them?'

'Not the stuff we've got. They're no good. All but the tigers are outlaws. But I do train them.'

'You like it?'

'Not much, the real big ones. But I like pumas. I'm going

to get an act together with them some time. But I'll need a lot of them. Jungle pumas. Not these outlaws you see in the zoos.'

'What's an outlaw?'

'He'd kill you.'

'Wouldn't they all?'

'They might, but an outlaw does anyhow. If it was people, he would be a crazy person. It comes from being bred in captivity. These cats you see, they look like cats, but they're really cat lunatics.'

'How can you tell it's a jungle cat?'

'I catch him in a jungle.'

'You mean you catch them *alive?*'

'Sure. They're no good to me dead.'

'Holy smoke. How do you do that?'

'Well, first I get on a boat and go down to Nicaragua. All the really fine pumas come from Nicaragua. These California and Mexican things are just scrubs compared to them. Then I hire me some Indian boys and go up in the mountains. Then I catch my pumas. Then I bring them back. But this time, I stay down there with them a while, to train them. Goat meat is cheaper there than horse meat is here.'

'You sound like you're all ready to start.'

'I am.'

She squirted a little wine in her mouth, and gave me a long look. They give it to you in a bottle with a long thin spout on it, and you squirt it in your mouth with the spout. That's to cool it. She did that two or three times, and every time she did it she would look at me.

'I am if you are.'

'What the hell? You think I'm going with you to catch them goddam things?'

'Frank, I brought quite a lot of money with me. Let's let Goebel keep those bughouse cats for their board, sell your car for whatever we can get, and hunt cats.'

'You're on.'

'You mean you will?'

'When do we start?'

'There's a freight boat out of here tomorrow and it puts in at Balboa. We'll wire Goebel from there. And we can leave your car with the hotel here. They'll sell it and send us whatever they get. That's one thing about a Mexican. He's slow, but he's honest.'

'OK.'

'Gee I'm glad.'

'Me too. I'm so sick of hot dogs and beer and apple pie with cheese on the side I could heave it all in the river.'

'You'll love it, Frank. We'll get a place up in the mountains, where it's cool, and then, after I get my act ready, we can go all over the world with it. Go as we please, do as we please, and have plenty of money to spend. Have you got a little bit of gypsy in you?'

'Gypsy? I had rings in my ears when I was born.'

I didn't sleep so good that night. When it was beginning to get light, I opened my eyes, wide awake. It came to me, then, that Nicaragua wouldn't be quite far enough.

14

When she got off the train she had on a black dress, that made her look tall, and a black hat, and black shoes and stockings, and didn't act like herself while the guy was loading the trunk in the car. We started out, and neither one of us had much to say for a few miles.

'Why didn't you let me know she died?'

'I didn't want to bother you with it. Anyhow, I had a lot to do.'

'I feel plenty bad now, Cora.'

'Why?'

'I took a trip while you were away. I went up to Frisco.'

'Why do you feel bad about that?'

'I don't know. You back there in Iowa, your mother dying and all, and me up in Frisco having a good time.'

'I don't know why you should feel bad. I'm glad you went. If I'd have thought about it, I'd have told you to before I left.'

'We lost some business. I closed down.'

'It's all right. We'll get it back.'

'I felt kind of restless, after you left.'

'Well my goodness, I don't mind.'

'I guess you had a bad time of it, hey?'

'It wasn't very pleasant. But anyhow, it's over.'

'I'll shoot a drink in you when we get home. I got some nice stuff out there I brought back to you.'

'I don't want any.'

'It'll pick you up.'

'I'm not drinking any more.'

'No?'

'I'll tell you about it. It's a long story.'

'You sound like plenty happened out there.'

'No, nothing happened. Only the funeral. But I've got a lot to tell you. I think we're going to have a better time of it from now on.'

'Well for God's sake. What is it?'

'Not now. Did you see your family?'

'What for?'

'Well anyway, did you have a good time?'

'Fair. Good as I could have alone.'

'I bet it was a swell time. But I'm glad you said it.'

When we got out there, a car was parked in front, and a guy was sitting in it. He got a silly kind of grin on his face and climbed out. It was Kennedy, the guy in Katz's office.

'You remember me?'

'Sure I remember you. Come on in.'

We took him inside, and she gave me a pull into the kitchen.

'This is bad, Frank.'

'What do you mean, bad?'

'I don't know, but I can feel it.'

'Better let me talk to him.'

I went back with him, and she brought us some beer, and left us, and pretty soon I got down to cases.

'You still with Katz?'

'No, I left him. We had a little argument and I walked out.'

'What are you doing now?'

'Not a thing. Fact of the matter, that's what I came out to see you about. I was out a couple of times before, but there was nobody home. This time, though, I heard you were back, so I stuck around.'

'Anything I can do, just say the word.'

'I was wondering if you could let me have a little money.'

'Anything you want. Of course, I don't keep much around, but if fifty or sixty dollars will help, I'll be glad to let you have it.'

'I was hoping you could make it more.'

He still had this grin on his face, and I figured it was time to quit the feinting and jabbing, and find out what he meant.

'Come on, Kennedy. What is it?'

'I tell you how it is. I left Katz. And that paper, the one I wrote up for Mrs Papadakis, was still in the files, see? And on account of being a friend of yours and all that, I knew you wouldn't want nothing like that laying around. So I took it. I thought maybe you would like to get it back.'

'You mean that hop dream she called a confession?'

'That's it. Of course, I know there wasn't anything to it, but I thought you might like to get it back.'

'How much do you want for it?'

'Well, how much would you pay?'

'Oh, I don't know. As you say, there's nothing to it, but I might give a hundred for it. Sure. I'd pay that.'

'I was thinking it was worth more.'

'Yeah?'

'I figured on twenty-five grand.'

'Are you crazy?'

'No, I ain't crazy. You got ten grand from Katz. The place has been making money, I figure about five grand. Then on the property, you could get ten grand from the bank. Papadakis gave fourteen for it, so it looked like you could get ten. Well, that makes twenty-five.'

'You would strip me clean, just for that?'

'It's worth it.'

I didn't move, but I must have had a flicker in my eye,

because he jerked an automatic out of his pocket and leveled it at me. 'Don't start anything, Chambers. In the first place, I haven't got it with me. In the second place, if you start anything I let you have it.'

'I'm not starting anything.'

'Well, see you don't.'

He kept the gun pointed at me, and I kept looking at him. 'I guess you got me.'

'I don't guess it. I know it.'

'But you're figuring too high.'

'Keep talking, Chambers.'

'We got ten from Katz, that's right. And we've still got it. We made five off the place, but we spent a grand in the last couple weeks. She took a trip to bury her mother, and I took one. That's why we been closed up.'

'Go on, keep talking.'

'And we can't get ten on the property. With things like they are now, we couldn't even get five. Maybe we could get four.'

'Keep talking.'

'All right, ten, four, and four. That makes eighteen.'

He grinned down the gun barrel a while, and then he got up. 'All right. Eighteen. I'll phone you tomorrow, to see if you've got it. If you've got it, I'll tell you what to do. If you haven't got it, that thing goes to Sackett.'

'It's tough, but you got me.'

'Tomorrow at twelve, then, I phone you. That'll give you time to go to the bank and get back.'

'OK.'

He backed to the door and still held the gun on me. It was late afternoon, just beginning to get dark. While he was backing away, I leaned up against the wall, like I was pretty down in the mouth. When he was half out the door I cut the juice in the sign, and it blazed down in his eyes. He wheeled, and I let him have it. He went down and I was on him. I twisted the gun out of his hand, threw it in the lunchroom, and socked him again. Then I dragged him inside and kicked the door shut. She was standing there. She had been at the door, listening, all the time.

'Get the gun.'

She picked it up and stood there. I pulled him to his feet, threw him over one of the tables, and bent him back. Then I beat him up. When he passed out, I got a glass of water and poured it on him. Soon as he came to, I beat him up again. When his face looked like raw beef, and he was blubbering like a kid in the last quarter of a football game, I quit.

'Snap out of it, Kennedy. You're talking to your friends over the telephone.'

'I got no friends, Chambers. I swear, I'm the only one that knows about—'

I let him have it, and we did it all over again. He kept saying he didn't have any friends, so I threw an arm lock on him and shoved up on it. 'All right, Kennedy. If you've got no friends, then I break it.'

He stood it longer than I thought he could. He stood it till I was straining on his arm with all I had, wondering if I really could break it. My left arm was still weak where it had been broke. If you ever tried to break the second joint of a tough turkey, maybe you know how hard it is to break a guy's arm with a hammerlock. But all of a sudden he said he would call. I let him loose and told him what he was to say. Then I put him at the kitchen phone, and pulled the lunchroom extension through the swing door, so I could watch him and hear what he said and they said. She came back there with us, with the gun.

'If I give you the sign, he gets it.'

She leaned back and an awful smile flickered around the corner of her mouth. I think that smile scared Kennedy worse than anything I had done.

'He gets it.'

He called, and a guy answered. 'Is that you, Willie?'

'Pat?'

'This is me. Listen. It's all fixed. How soon can you get out here with it?'

'Tomorrow, like we said.'

'Can't you make it tonight?'

'How can I get in a safe deposit box when the bank is closed?'

'All right, then do like I tell you. Get it, first thing in the morning, and come out here with it. I'm out to his place.'

'His *place*?'

'Listen, get this, Willie. He knows we got him, see? But he's afraid if she finds out he's got to pay all that dough, she won't let him, you get it? If he leaves, she knows something is up, and maybe she takes a notion to go with him. So we do it all here. I'm just a guy that's spending the night in their auto camp, and she don't know nothing. Tomorrow, you're just a friend of mine, and we fix it all up.'

'How does he get the money if he don't leave?'

'That's all fixed up.'

'And what in the hell are you spending the night there for?'

'I got a reason for that, Willie. Because maybe it's a stall, what he says about her, and maybe it's not, see? But if I'm here, neither one of them can skip, you get it?'

'Can he hear you, what you're saying?'

He looked at me, and I nodded my head yes. 'He's right here with me, in the phone booth. I want him to hear me, you get it, Willie? I want him to know we mean business.'

'It's a funny way to do, Pat.'

'Listen, Willie. You don't know, and I don't know, and none of us don't know if he's on the level with it or not. But maybe he is, and I'm giving him a chance. What the hell, if a guy's willing to pay, we got to go along with him, haven't we? That's it. You do like I tell you. You get it out here soon as you can in the morning. Soon as you can, you get it? Because I don't want her to get to wondering what the hell I'm doing hanging around here all day.'

'OK.'

He hung up. I walked over and gave him a sock. 'That's just so you talk right when he calls back. You got it, Kennedy?'

'I got it.'

I waited a few minutes, and pretty soon here came the call back. I answered, and when Kennedy picked up the phone he gave Willie some more of the same. He said he was alone that time. Willie didn't like it much, but he had to take it. Then I took him back to the No. 1 shack. She came with us, and I took the gun. Soon as I had Kennedy inside, I stepped out the door with her and gave her a kiss.

'That's for being able to step on it when the pinch comes. Now get this. I'm not leaving him for a minute. I'm staying out here the whole night. There'll be other calls, and we'll bring him in to talk. I think you better open the place up. The beer garden. Don't bring anybody inside. That's so if his friends do some spying, you're right on deck and it's business as usual.'

'All right. And Frank.'

'Yes?'

'Next time I try to act smart, will you hang one on my jaw?'

'What do you mean?'

'We ought to have gone away. Now I know it.'

'Like hell we ought. Not till we get this.'

She gave me a kiss, then. 'I guess I like you pretty well, Frank.'

'We'll get it. Don't worry.'

'I'm not.'

I stayed out there with him all night. I didn't give him any food, and I didn't give him any sleep. Three or four times he had to talk to Willie, and once Willie wanted to talk to me. Near as I could tell, we got away with it. In between, I would beat him up. It was hard work, but I meant he should want that paper to get there, bad. While he was wiping the blood off his face, on a towel, you could hear the radio going, out in the beer garden, and people laughing and talking.

About ten o'clock the next morning she came out there. 'They're here, I think. There are three of them.'

'Bring them back.'

She picked up the gun, stuck it in her belt so you couldn't see it from in front, and went. In a minute, I heard something fall. It was one of his gorillas. She was marching them in front of her, making them walk backwards with their hands up, and one of them fell when his heel hit the concrete walk. I opened the door. 'This way, gents.'

They came in, still holding their hands up, and she came in after them and handed me the gun. 'They all had guns, but I took them off them in the lunchroom.'

'Better get them. Maybe they got friends.'

She went, and in a minute came back with the guns. She took out the clips, and laid them on the bed, beside me. Then she went through their pockets. Pretty soon she had it. And the funny part was that in another envelope were photostats of it, six positives and one negative. They had meant to keep on blackmailing us, and then hadn't had any more sense than to have the photostats on them when they showed up. I took them all, with the original, outside, crumpled them up on the ground, and touched a match to them. When they were burned I stamped the ashes into the dirt and went back.

'All right, boys. I'll show you out. We'll keep the artillery here.'

After I had marched them out to their cars, and they left, and I went back inside, she wasn't there. I went out back, and she wasn't there. I went upstairs. She was in our room. 'Well, we did it, didn't we? That's the last of it, photostats and all. It's been worrying me, too.'

She didn't say anything, and her eyes looked funny. 'What's the matter, Cora?'

'So that's the last of it, is it? Photostats and all. It isn't the last of me, though. I've got a million photostats of it, just as good as they were. Jimmy Durante. I've got a million of them. Am I mortified?'

She burst out laughing, and flopped down on the bed.

'All right. If you're sucker enough to put your neck in the noose, just to get me, you've got a million of them. You sure have. A million of them.'

'Oh, no, that's the beautiful part. I don't have to put my neck in the noose at all. Didn't Mr Katz tell you? Once they just made it manslaughter, they can't do any more to me. It's in the Constitution or something. Oh no, Mr Frank Chambers. It don't cost me a thing to make you dance on air. And that's what you're going to do. Dance, dance, dance.'

'What ails you, anyhow?'

'Don't you know? Your friend was out last night. She didn't know about me, and she spent the night here.'

'What friend?'

'The one you went to Mexico with. She told me all about it. We're good friends now. She thought we better be good friends. After she found out who I was she thought I might kill her.'

'I haven't been to Mexico for a year.'

'Oh yes you have.'

She went out, and I heard her go in my room. When she came back she had a kitten with her, but a kitten that was bigger than a cat. It was gray, with spots on it. She put it on the table in front of me and it began to meow. 'The puma had little ones while you were gone, and she brought you one to remember her by.'

She leaned back against the wall and began to laugh again, a wild, crazy laugh. 'And the cat came back! It stepped on the fuse box and got killed, but here it is back! Ha, ha, ha, ha, ha, ha! Ain't that funny, how unlucky cats are for you?'

15

S he cracked up, then, and cried, and after she got quiet she went downstairs. I was down there, right after her. She was tearing the top flaps off a big carton.

'Just making a nest for our little pet, dearie.'

'Nice of you.'

'What did you think I was doing?'

'I didn't.'

'Don't worry. When the time comes to call up Mr Sackett, I'll let you know. Just take it easy. You'll need all your strength.'

She lined it with excelsior, and on top of that put some woolen cloths. She took it upstairs and put the puma in it. It meowed a while and then went to sleep. I went downstairs to fix myself a coke. I hadn't any more than squirted the ammonia in it than she was at the door.

'Just taking something to keep my strength up, dearie.'

'Nice of you.'

'What did you think I was doing?'

'I didn't.'

'Don't worry. When I get ready to skip I'll let you know. Just take it easy. You may need all your strength.'

She gave me a funny look and went upstairs. It kept up all day, me following her around for fear she'd call up Sackett, her following me around for fear I'd skip. We never opened the place up at all. In between the tip-toeing around, we would sit upstairs in the room. We didn't look at each other. We looked at the puma. It would meow and she would go down to get it some milk. I would go with her. After it lapped up the milk it would go to sleep. It was too young to play much. Most of the time it meowed or slept.

That night we lay side by side, not saying a word. I must have slept, because I had those dreams. Then, all of a sudden, I woke up, and before I was even really awake I was running downstairs. What had waked me was the sound of that telephone dial. She was at the extension in the lunchroom, all dressed, with her hat on, and a packed hat box on the floor beside her. I grabbed the receiver and slammed it on the hook. I took her by the shoulders, jerked her through the swing door, and shoved her upstairs. 'Get up there! Get up there, or I'll—'

'Or you'll what?'

The telephone rang, and I answered it.

'Here's your party, go ahead.'

'Yellow Cab.'

'Oh. Oh. I called you, Yellow Cab, but I've changed my mind. I won't need you.'

'OK.'

When I got upstairs she was taking off her clothes. When we got back in bed we lay there a long time again without saying a word. Then she started up.

'Or you'll what?'

'What's it to you? Sock you in the jaw, maybe. Maybe something else.'

'Something else, wasn't it?'

'What are you getting at now?'

'Frank, I know what you've been doing. You've been lying there, trying to think of a way to kill me.'

'I've been asleep.'

'Don't lie to me, Frank. Because I'm not going to lie to you, and I've got something to say to you.'

I thought that over a long time. Because that was just what I had been doing. Lying there beside her, just straining to think of a way I could kill her.

'All right, then. I was.'

'I knew it.'

'Were you any better? Weren't you going to hand me over to Sackett? Wasn't that the same thing?'

'Yes.'

'Then we're even. Even again. Right back where we started.'

'Not quite.'

'Oh yes we are.' I cracked up a little, then, myself, and put my head on her shoulder. 'That's just where we are. We can kid ourself all we want to, and laugh about the money, and whoop about what a swell guy the devil is to be in bed with, but that's just where we are. I was going off with that woman, Cora. We were going to Nicaragua to catch cats. And why I didn't go away, I knew I had to come back. We're chained to each other, Cora. We thought we were on top of a mountain. That wasn't it. It's on top of us, and that's where it's been ever since that night.'

'Is that the only reason you came back?'

'No. It's you and me. There's nobody else. I love you, Cora. But love, when you get fear in it, it's not love any more. It's hate.'

'So you hate me?'

'I don't know. But we're telling the truth, for once in our life. That's part of it. You got to know it. And what I was lying here thinking, that's the reason. Now you know it.'

'I told you I had something to tell you, Frank.'

'Oh.'

'I'm going to have a baby.'

'*What?*'

'I suspicioned it before I went away, and right after my mother died I was sure.'

'The hell you say. The hell you say. Come here. Give me a kiss.'

'No. Please. I've got to tell you about it.'

'Haven't you told it?'

'Not what I mean. Now listen to me, Frank. All that time I was out there, waiting for the funeral to be over, I thought about it. What it would mean to us. Because we took a life, didn't we? And now we're going to give one back.'

'That's right.'

'It was all mixed up, what I thought. But now, after what happened with that woman, it's not mixed up any more. I couldn't call up Sackett, Frank. I couldn't call him up, because I couldn't have this baby, and then have it find out I let its father hang for murder.'

'You were going to see Sackett.'

'No I wasn't. I was going away.'

'Was that the only reason you weren't going to see Sackett?'

She took a long time before she answered that. 'No. I love you, Frank. I think you know that. But maybe, if it hadn't been for this, I would have gone to see him. Just *because* I love you.'

'She didn't mean anything to me, Cora. I told you why I did it. I was running away.'

'I know that. I knew it all along. I knew why you wanted to take me away, and what I said about you being a bum, I didn't believe that. I believed it, but it wasn't why you wanted to go. You being a bum, I love you for it. And I hated her for the way she turned on you just for not telling her about something that wasn't any of her business. And yet, I wanted to ruin you for it.'

'Well?'

'I'm trying to say it, Frank. This is what I'm trying to say. I wanted to ruin you, and yet I couldn't go to see Sackett. It wasn't because you kept watching me. I could have run out of the house and got to him. It was because, like I told you. Well then, I'm rid of the devil, Frank. I know I'll never call up Sackett, because I had my chance, and I had my reason, and I didn't do it. So the devil has left me. But has he left you?'

'If he's left you, then what more have I got to do with him?'

'We wouldn't be sure. We couldn't ever be sure unless you had your chance. The same chance I had.'

'I tell you, he's gone.'

'While you were thinking about a way to kill me, Frank, I was thinking the same thing. Of a way you could kill me. You can kill me swimming. We'll go way out, the way we did last time, and if you don't want me to come back, you don't have to let me. Nobody'll ever know. It'll be just one of those things that happen at the beach. Tomorrow morning we'll go.'

'Tomorrow morning, what we do is get married.'

'We can get married if you want, but before we come back we go swimming.'

'To hell with swimming. Come on with that kiss.'

'Tomorrow night, if I come back, there'll be kisses. Lovely ones, Frank. Not drunken kisses. Kisses with dreams in them. Kisses that come from life, not death.'

'It's a date.'

We got married at the City Hall, and then we went to the beach. She looked so pretty I just wanted to play in the sand with her, but she had this little smile on her face, and after a while she got up and went down to the surf.

'I'm going out.'

She went ahead, and I swam after her. She kept on going, and went a lot further out than she had before. Then she stopped, and I caught up with her. She swung up beside me, and took hold of my hand, and we looked at each other. She knew, then, that the devil was gone, that I loved her.

'Did I ever tell you why I like my feet to the swells?'

'No.'

'It's so they'll lift them.'

A big one raised us up, and she put her hand to her breasts, to show how it lifted them. 'I love it. Are they big, Frank?'

'I'll tell you tonight.'

'They feel big. I didn't tell you about that. It's not only knowing you're going to make another life. It's what it does to you. My breasts feel so big, and I want you to kiss them. Pretty soon my belly is going to get big, and I'll love that, and want everybody to see it. It's life. I can feel it in me. It's a new life for us both, Frank.'

We started back, and on the way in I swam down. I went down nine feet. I could tell it was nine feet, by the pressure. Most of these pools are nine feet, and it was that deep. I whipped my legs together and shot down further. It drove in on my ears so I thought they would pop. But I didn't have to come up. The pressure on your lungs drives the oxygen in your blood, so for a few seconds you don't think about breath. I looked at the green water. And with my ears ringing and that weight on my back and chest, it seemed to me that all the devilment, and meanness, and shiftlessness, and no-account stuff in my life had been pressed out and washed off, and I was all ready to start out with her again clean, and do like she said, have a new life.

When I came up she was coughing. 'Just one of those sick spells, like you have.'

'Are you all right?'

'I think so. It comes over you, and then it goes.'

'Did you swallow any water?'

'No.'

We went a little way, and then she stopped. 'Frank, I feel funny inside.'

'Here, hold on to me.'

'Oh, Frank. Maybe I strained myself, just then. Trying to keep my head up. So I wouldn't gulp down the salt water.'

'Take it easy.'

'Wouldn't that be awful? I've heard of women that had a miscarriage. From straining theirself.'

'Take it easy. Lie right out in the water. Don't try to swim. I'll tow you in.'

'Hadn't you better call a guard?'

'Christ no. That egg will want to pump your legs up and down. Just lay there now. I'll get you in quicker than he can.'

She lay there, and I towed her by the shoulder strap of her bathing suit. I began to give out. I could have towed her a mile, but I kept thinking I had to get her to a hospital, and I hurried. When you hurry in the water you're sunk. I got bottom, though, after a while, and then I took her in my arms and rushed her through the surf. 'Don't move. Let me do it.'

'I won't.'

I ran with her up to the place where our sweaters were, and set her down. I got the car key out of mine, then wrapped both of them around her and carried her up to the car. It was up beside the road, and I had to climb the high bank the road was on, above the beach. My legs were so tired I could hardly lift one after the other, but I didn't drop her. I put her in the car, started up, and began burning the road.

We had gone in swimming a couple of miles above Santa Monica, and there was a hospital down there. I overtook a big truck. It had a sign on the back, Sound Your Horn, the Road Is Yours. I banged on the horn, and it kept right down the middle. I couldn't pass on the left, because a whole line of cars was coming toward me. I pulled out to the right and stepped on it. She screamed. I never saw the culvert wall. There was a crash, and everything went black.

When I came out of it I was wedged down beside the wheel, with my back to the front of the car, but I began to moan from the awfulness of what I heard. It was like rain on a tin roof, but that wasn't it. It was her blood, pouring down on the hood, where she went through the windshield. Horns were blowing, and people were jumping out of cars and running to her. I got her up, and tried to stop the blood and in between I was talking to her, and crying, and kissing her. Those kisses never reached her. She was dead.

16

They got me for it. Katz took it all this time, the $10,000 he had got for us, and the money we had made, and a deed for the place. He did his best for me, but he was licked from the start. Sackett said I was a mad dog, that had to be put out of the way before life would be safe. He had it all figured out. We murdered the Greek to get the money, and then I married her, and murdered her so I could have it all myself. When she found out about the Mexican trip, that hurried it up a little, that was all. He had the autopsy report, that showed she was going to have a baby, and he said that was part of it. He put Madge on the stand, and she told about the Mexican trip. She didn't want to, but she had to. He even had the puma in court. It had grown, but it hadn't been taken care of right, so it was mangy and sick looking, and yowled, and tried to bite him. It was an awful looking thing, and it didn't do me any good, believe me. But what really sunk me was the note she wrote before she called up the cab, and put in the cash register so I would get it in the morning, and then forgot about. I never saw it, because we didn't open the place before we went swimming, and I never even looked in the cash register. It was the sweetest note in the world, but it had in it about us killing the Greek, and that did the work. They argued about it three days, and Katz fought them with every law book in Los Angeles County, but the judge let it in, and that let in all about us murdering the Greek. Sackett said that fixed me up with a motive. That and just being a mad dog. Katz never even let me take the stand. What could I say? That I didn't do it, because we had just fixed it up, all the trouble we had had over killing the Greek? That would have been swell. The jury was out five minutes. The judge said he would give me exactly the same consideration he would show any other mad dog.

So I'm in the death house, now, writing the last of this, so Father McConnell can look it over and show me the places where maybe it ought to be fixed up a little, for punctuation and all that. If I get a stay, he's to hold on to it and wait for what happens. If I get a commutation, then, he's to burn it, and they'll never know whether there really was any murder or not, from anything I tell them. But if they get me, he's to take it and see if he can find somebody to print it. There won't be any stay, and there won't be any commutation, I know that. I never kidded myself. But in this place, you hope anyhow, just because you can't help it. I never confessed anything, that's one thing. I heard a guy say they never hang you without you confess. I don't know. Unless Father McConnell crosses me, they'll never know anything from me. Maybe I'll get a stay.

I'm getting up tight now, and I've been thinking about Cora. Do you think she knows I didn't do it? After what we said in the water, you would think she would know it. But that's the awful part, when you monkey with murder. Maybe it went through her head, when the car hit, that I did it anyhow. That's why I hope I've got another life after this one. Father McConnell says I have, and I want to see her. I want her to know that it was all so, what we said to each other, and that I didn't do it. What did she have that makes me feel that way about her? I don't know. She wanted something, and she tried to get it. She tried all the wrong ways, but she tried. I don't know what made her feel that way about me, because she knew me. She called it on me plenty of times, that I wasn't any good. I never really wanted anything, but her. But that's a lot. I guess it's not often that a woman even has that.

There's a guy in No. 7 that murdered his brother, and says he didn't really do it, his subconscious did it. I asked him what that meant, and he says you got two selves, one that you know about and the other that you don't know about, because it's subconscious. It shook me up. Did I really do it, and not know it? God Almighty, I can't believe that! I didn't do it! I loved her so, then, I tell you, that I would have died for her! To hell with the subconscious. I don't believe it. It's just a lot of hooey, that this guy thought up so he could fool the judge. You know what you're doing, and you do it. I didn't do it, I know that. That's what I'm going to tell her, if I ever see her again.

I'm up awful tight, now. I think they give you dope in the grub, so you don't think about it. I try not to think. Whenever I can make it, I'm out there with Cora, with the sky above us, and the water around us, talking about how happy we're going to be, and how it's going to last forever. I guess I'm over the big river, when I'm there with her. That's when it seems real, about another life, not with all this stuff how Father McConnell has got it figured out. When I'm with her I believe it. When I start to figure, it all goes blooey.

No stay.

Here they come. Father McConnell says prayers help. If you've got this far, send up one for me, and Cora, and make it that we're together, wherever it is.

available from

THE ORION PUBLISHING GROUP

☐ **Do Androids Dream of Electric Sheep?** £6.99
PHILIP K. DICK
0 75286 430 0

☐ **Double Indemnity** £6.99
JAMES M. CAIN
0 75286 427 0

☐ **Hombre** £6.99
ELMORE LEONARD
0 75286 437 8

☐ **Minority Report** £6.99
PHILIP K. DICK
0 75286 431 9

☐ **Terms of Endearment** £6.99
LARRY MCMURTRY
0 75286 448 3

☐ **The Bourne Identity** £6.99
ROBERT LUDLUM
0 75286 432 7

☐ **The Color Purple** £6.99
ALICE WALKER
0 75286 434 3

☐ **The Getaway** £6.99
JIM THOMPSON
0 75286 435 1

☐ **The Green Mile** £6.99
STEPHEN KING
0 75286 433 5

☐ **The Grifters** £6.99
JIM THOMPSON
0 75286 428 9

☐ **The Hound of the Baskervilles** £6.99
SIR ARTHUR CONAN DOYLE
0 75286 460 2

☐ **The Maltese Falcon** £6.99
DASHIELL HAMMETT
0 75286 533 1

☐ **The Pianist** £6.99
WLADYSLAW SZPILMAN
0 75286 429 7

☐ **The Postman Always Rings Twice** £6.99
JAMES M. CAIN
0 75286 436 X

☐ **Valdez is Coming** £6.99
ELMORE LEONARD
0 75286 449 1

All Orion/Phoenix titles are available at your local bookshop or from the following address:

Mail Order Department
Littlehampton Book Services
FREEPOST BR535
Worthing, West Sussex, BN13 3BR
telephone 01903 828503, *facsimile* 01903 828802
e-mail MailOrders@lbsltd.co.uk
(Please ensure that you include full postal address details)

Payment can be made either by credit/debit card (Visa, Mastercard, Access and Switch accepted) or by sending a £ Sterling cheque or postal order made payable to *Littlehampton Book Services*.
DO NOT SEND CASH OR CURRENCY.

Please add the following to cover postage and packing

UK and BFPO:
£1.50 for the first book, and 50p for each additional book to a maximum of £3.50

Overseas and Eire:
£2.50 for the first book plus £1.00 for the second book and 50p for each additional book ordered

---

BLOCK CAPITALS PLEASE

name of cardholder ....

address of cardholder ....

delivery address
(if different from cardholder)
....
....
....
....

postcode ....   *postcode* ....

[ ] I enclose my remittance for £............................

[ ] please debit my Mastercard/Visa/Access/Switch (delete as appropriate)

card number [ ][ ][ ][ ][ ][ ][ ][ ][ ][ ][ ][ ][ ][ ][ ][ ]

expiry date [ ][ ][ ][ ]   Switch issue no. [ ][ ]

signature ....

prices and availability are subject to change without notice